I0627130
Black
Fern

THE ANTHOLOGY OF EROTIC NARRATIVE

VOLUME II

POCKETBOOK EDITION

INTERNATIONAL AUTHORS

DANTE REMY
EDITOR

Black Fern

Copyright 2025 Erosetti Press

ISBN 978-1-968703-03-5

Pocketbook Edition

Black Fern, an imprint of Erosetti Press,
publishes classic and contemporary erotic novels
that transcend boundaries and
explore the depths of human desire.

CONTENTS

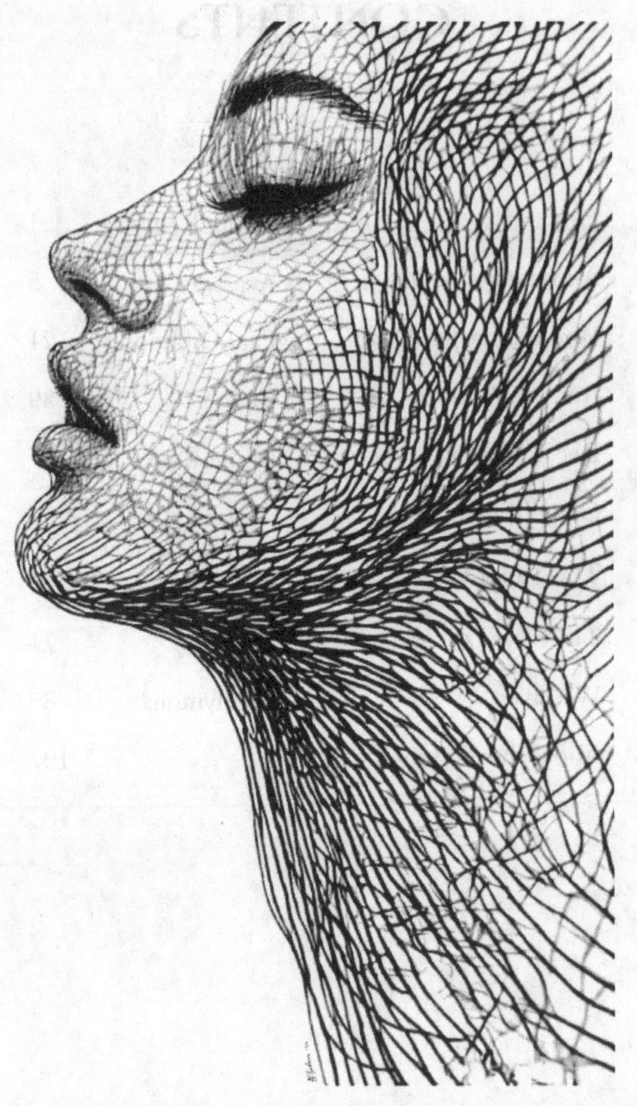

FORWARD

What is erotic narrative,
if not the pulse beneath the page?
A rhythm we read,
not just with our eyes,
but with everything we are.

Erotic narrative is no mere indulgence. It is the friction between repression and revelation, between the conscious and the primal, between the sacred and the obscene. To write erotica is to trace the edge of being—with blood, breath, sweat, and soul. This anthology, *The Anthology of Erotic Narrative, Volume II*, is not a collection of fantasies alone. It is a map of the body and a mirror of the mind, rendered in ink and instinct.

The stories gathered in this *Pocketbook Edition* are incandescent with tension, the layout balanced by the illustrations of A.V. Budkin, who agreed to renumeration in Negronis and drinks made from medicinal gin. The *Illustrated Edition* of the anthology features the unmistakable black-and-white work of Ester Cardella— an Italian illustrator and comics artist renowned for her evocative blend of eroticism, horror, and feminist themes. Her "erotic and heretic" vision (as she once described it) electrifies the pages of the volume with bold lines, transgressive beauty, and sacred indecency. Cardella's illustrations are not adornments, but eruptions: capturing longing in a parted mouth, power in the grip of a thigh, or the abyssal knowing in the shadowed gaze of a woman atop her lover. Her drawings, like the stories in this volume, are sites of seduction, worship, and resistance. You will find the uncensored *Illustrated Edition* on the Erosetti Press website in deluxe hardcover and paperback.

We begin with Ava Lee's *A Friendly Gangbang*, a daring act of devotion where the protagonist, blindfolded and bound, embraces her desires among friends in a consensual celebration of power and submission. It is not the act itself that defines her but her control of it—her body as altar and weapon, her pleasure not taken, but claimed.

We next step into the sapphic tension of Paul Gibbons' *Wrestling with Desire*, where play-fighting between girlfriends becomes a contest of control, trust, and unchecked lust. Lyra, pinned and trembling beneath Penny's strength, discovers the exquisite loss of power in being broken open—by cruelty, but by love. The story balances erotic humor and vulnerability with a tender ferocity that only WLW narratives dare explore so fully.

An Artist's Muse by Tiggs reminds us that sometimes the most dangerous seductions are wordless. A painter and his model blur the line between voyeur and exhibitionist, creator and subject.

With each stroke of the brush and gaze held too long, art becomes foreplay and confession. The body becomes a palette; the canvas becomes confession.

In *Reconciliation* by Dante Remy, the ritual of return—of ex-lovers circling back through memory, indiscretion, and lust— becomes a form of absolution. Grief, guilt, and grace twist together as bodies intertwine and old wounds reopen beneath the skin, only to be licked shut. It is a story of reckoning and resurrection, and of what it means to forgive through flesh.

The anonymous narrator in *Casual Encounters* by Artgasim enters a transactional arrangement with startling emotional depth. Blurring pornographic intensity with psychological insight, it invites readers to consider who holds the power when desire is mutual, boundaries are clear, and expectations are turned inside out. It's a theater of the erotic where trust is the script and dominance is shared.

The Taxi Driver by Looking for Illustrator brings the perspective back to the confident, elegantly dressed wife who orchestrates a bold, dominant tryst in the back of a taxi. She is not broken, not searching — she is sovereign. She controls her sexuality the way she controls the driver's gaze and the night itself: by unbuttoning it slowly, daring the world to watch. It's told from her point of view, unapologetically female and deliberate in its charge.

Then comes *The Sleaze and the Stoic* by JK Mill—a brutal yet redemptive dive into blackmail, degradation, and the sliver of salvation offered by an unexpected witness. D, the narrator, is thrust into an arranged encounter with two men— one grotesque and boastful, the other silent and solemn. What begins in coercion turns to something close to care as the stoic man later protects her, comforts her, and offers escape from a trap sprung by faceless cruelty. The story has teeth and tenderness in equal measure.

And finally, we descend—or ascend—into the fever-dream of *We Live* by Anonymous: an apocalyptic ode to lust, biology, and survival. Harissa, a woman of the new world, finds Vanko, a man of the old. Their days are a relentless blur of sex, not out of indulgence but necessity—a ritual to resurrect life itself. "Sterling sperm finding its queen egg," she says, in a climax that feels like prophecy. Here, orgasm is religion; bodies are battlegrounds; the last moan is a war cry.

These tales insist that desire is not decoration— it is declaration. Eroticism is not always gentle. It disturbs. It reveals. It strips us bare, not just of clothes but of illusions, language, even time. These stories do not ask for permission—they offer invitation.

Erotic narrative is honest enough
to let the soul tremble—
freed from the restraints of shame,
undone by longing, revealed in sacred lust.
It does not ask to cleanse us,
but to awaken us—
whole and human, in flesh and in shadow.

Come closer. Turn the page. Let yourself be taken.

—Dante Remy

A FRIENDLY GANGBANG

BY AVA LEE

Keywords: Fsub, fantasy-empowerment, anticipation, established relationship, friends-to-lovers, wifesharing, free-use, gangbang, restraints, gentle & rough, aftercare.

Synopsis: A woman realizes her deepest fantasy of a consensual gangbang with her partner's support. Blindfolded and restrained, she explores her vulnerability and sexual boundaries, embracing the tension between objectification and self-possession. Surrounded by trusted friends, she revels in the power of her choices, experiencing both tenderness and roughness on her terms. With ongoing consent and aftercare, she transforms the experience into a celebration of her sexuality and autonomy, fully realizing her desires and deepening her connection with her partner.

A FRIENDLY GANGBANG

Another shiver of excitement runs through my body—and they haven't even begun. I'm still alone in the room, sure of it despite the snug blindfold that reduces my world to velvet darkness. As always, the loss of sight heightens my awareness of my body. I'm completely naked, the sheets soft and cool beneath my skin, my head and upper back propped up by a large cushion. My movements are limited but not fully restricted. When I pull, I feel the soft pressure of the restraints on my wrists and ankles. My hands are tied together to the headboard, my legs spread, each foot bound to a bedpost. The restraints are loose enough to let me bend my knees, but tight enough to give me that delicious sense of helplessness, of vulnerability.

I love being bound so tight I can't move a limb, but today is different. These restraints allow a level of comfort—because I'll be here for hours. I'll be not just his to use, but theirs. Their fucktoy. Their free-use slut for the night. Ready to be taken whenever they feel the urge—gentle or rough. One after the other, or two or three at once. How many are there, anyway? I strain to listen, but I can't make out their voices from the living room downstairs, just the sound of a football match on TV, laughter, the clink of bottles. He wouldn't invite strangers, but I don't know who of our friends and acquaintances came to this unconventional gathering. It hits me: I won't know who sees me like this. Who touches me. Who will be inside me in the next few minutes. The thought is equally terrifying and arousing. My pussy twitches with need. My nipples harden almost to the point of pain, goosebumps prickling around them. My heart races. The anticipation is unbearable.

Footsteps approach. I hold my breath. I've never felt so naked. Just one person, I realize. Then I catch the scent of his cologne. My partner, my love. He sits quietly beside me on the bed, and some of the tension fades. Still, I flinch when he touches my thigh; I didn't see it coming. "You look absolutely delicious," he whispers. "I'm just checking in before we start. How are you feeling?"

I'm feeling so many things at once—excitement, arousal, vulnerability. Gratitude that he made this happen. A friendly gangbang has been a fantasy of mine for ages, and I know he wasn't always keen on the idea, let alone the challenge of organizing it with the right people. Close enough to feel safe, distant enough to avoid awkward encounters later. Over time, we built a circle of what we affectionately called our 'slut friends': actors, nude photographers, fellow writers of erotica, people we met at kink events. Open-minded, but still, fucking in front of others is different. At least being tied up in a separate room eases some of the pressure. I can be alone with each of them, maybe even experience tenderness. Or they could come at me all at once and push my limits. It's a gangbang, after all.

I'm seeking that delicate balance between intimacy and depravity, being objectified yet cherished. Is that even possible? How much can I handle? Now that my fantasy is about to become reality, nervousness mixes with the thrill, threatening to spill into fear.

He senses it. He admits he's nervous too, but not as much as he expected. The guys are excited, he says, but not in a competitive way. "They know this has been your dream for nearly a decade, and they want to make it amazing for you. Apparently, you've told some of them about it in detail." I remember those conversations—testing the waters, gauging reactions, secretly hoping to draw the intrigued into the fantasy.

He kisses my forehead. "You can call this off anytime, even now," he says. "I can untie you, we can greet everyone, and let it unfold more naturally. You don't have to fuck anyone—they'd understand if your nerves took over."

I breathe deeply, slowly exhaling. I needed to hear that, to make this choice consciously all over again. "No," I say. "I trust you. I want this."

"Good," he growls. "You can't see it, but I'm rock hard. I had my doubts, but now all I want is to see you get fucked by multiple men." His words crank my arousal to another level. Wifesharing has always been a kink of mine, and I've been impatient for him to open up to it. He kisses me possessively, cupping my pussy at the same time. I can't wait for this to begin. "Who's downstairs?" I ask, breathless. His grin is audible. "Oh, I'm not telling you. But I'll send them in, one by one, to say hi."

And with that, he leaves me alone in velvet darkness once more.

Time blurs when blindfolded. Minutes stretch like hours. I can hear voices but not make out words. Is he giving instructions, or are they still talking about the match? I run through the guest list in my mind again and again. It's nerve-wracking not to know. Finally, footsteps in the hall. True to his promise, he sends them in separately to greet me. They're sweet, checking my consent, telling me they've all done STD tests and shared results with my partner. Each man tells me how hot I look, hints at what they're going to do later. They caress me, kiss me, but none of them touches my intimate parts. By the third visitor, it's clear they agreed to this beforehand—to make me feel safe first. It's working, even though I can't be certain I've identified all my visitors. Two are familiar; we've been intimate before. The other two remain a mystery, though I think I can guess from their voices and mannerisms.

When the fifth man enters, it's my partner again. By now, my whole body is buzzing with anticipation, and I barely let him finish asking if I'm ready to move forward. He chuckles at my eagerness. "From now on," he says, "you're fair game."

Then: nothing. Laughter and chatter drift in from the living room, but no one comes in for what feels like forever. Are they waiting on purpose to build tension, or easing into this new setting themselves? Just when insecurity starts creeping in, the door opens. Footsteps, breathing, then the soft scratch of a beard on my inner thigh. He doesn't speak but kisses his way slowly, teasingly, towards my pussy. A needy moan escapes me, met with a bemused chuckle. We haven't even exchanged words, yet his tongue is the first part of him inside me. But I never said my fantasies were mainstream. When his tongue finally reaches its destination, it's bliss. Slow and sensual, yet eager. I'm so close to the edge, but he doesn't let me tip over, moving on before I can climax. A few kisses on my breasts, and he's gone again.

I squirm in my restraints, aching for release. Before long, the next visitor arrives. A familiar deep voice murmurs, "I've missed touching you like this." He stretches out beside me, his bulge pressing against my hip. I hope to feel him inside me tonight, and I tell him so. He grins. "Needy, aren't you?" But I know he loves needy. His fingers explore my body, mixing praise with dirty talk. When he calls me a little slut and slips a finger inside, I moan in response, already dripping. His finger slides deeper, curling just right, and he chuckles as he feels how wet I am. "I brought lube," he teases, "but I don't think we'll need it."

I gasp, arching into his touch, desperate for more. "Maybe someone's in the mood for anal," I suggest breathlessly, feeling bold.

He laughs softly, and I hear him shift beside me. "We were actually talking about that in the living room," he confesses. His finger continues to play inside me, pushing me closer to the edge, but he stops after a few short, torturous minutes. "Not yet, though. There are others waiting," he says, pulling away and leaving me empty, needy, and desperate.

I barely have time to process the loss before the next man enters. This one moves quietly, his presence felt more than heard. He stands by the bed for a moment, letting me squirm in my restraints, soaking in my vulnerability. Then, unexpectedly, he kisses my lips. His kiss is slow and teasing, full of promises. My heart races. He moves to my neck, planting soft, lingering kisses that send shivers down my spine.

His mouth finds my nipple, tongue circling it with agonizing precision, while his fingers pinch the other, sending jolts of pleasure-pain through my body. I gasp and moan, writhing under his touch, lost in the mix of pleasure and torment. He slaps my pussy lightly, alternating with soft licks, driving me wild with need. "Who is this perfect stranger, this gentle sadist?" I wonder. I have an idea of who he is, but I can't quite believe he's here, indulging in my fantasy. He keeps me on edge, never letting me reach that final release.

Just as I'm about to beg, two more sets of footsteps approach. My body trembles as they reach the bed, each taking a side. Their hands are on me instantly—familiar, confident touches. One pair grabs my breast, squeezing, kneading, while the other traces my inner thigh. I smile despite myself. It's no surprise these two came in together. They've always had good chemistry, and this isn't the first time we've shared a bed. Their hands roam, fingers trailing across my skin, stroking, exploring.

I feel so shared, so desired. It's intoxicating.

They move in sync, pulling my legs apart. I can feel their breath on me, the anticipation building. One slides a finger inside me, slow and deliberate, while the other teases my clit, circling lazily. My back arches, my body responding immediately. They know exactly how to touch me, hitting all the right spots, teasing me closer and closer to the edge. My breathing becomes erratic as I beg them to speed up, desperate for release.

But they only chuckle, slowing down their movements instead. I whimper in frustration, the denial of pleasure almost unbearable. They are toying with me, keeping me on the brink of orgasm, never letting me fall over. I'm begging them now, my voice trembling. "Please, please let me cum!"

They don't. They continue their slow, torturous rhythm, taking their time, savoring every reaction. Their lips are on my nipples now, their tongues flicking and sucking as they tease me mercilessly. Every nerve in my body is on fire, desperate for release.

Suddenly, I feel more hands. They're everywhere—on my thighs, my breasts, my neck, my mouth. The others have joined, surrounding me, their lips and hands exploring every inch of my body. I'm overwhelmed by the sheer intensity of it all—the weight of their touch, the heat of their breath, the raw, primal desire radiating from them.

I can feel a familiar beard brushing against my inner thigh again. He's back. I know what's coming, and the anticipation makes me tremble. His hot breath teases my clit, and I think I might lose my mind. Fingers—three, maybe four—slide inside me, stretching me, filling me, and I moan loudly as pleasure crashes over me.

And then, finally, his tongue. It's like lightning striking my clit, each flick sending shockwaves through my body. There's no holding back now—my orgasm hits me like a tidal wave, ripping through me with a force I've never felt before. I scream, my body convulsing as wave after wave of pleasure crashes over me, through me, drowning me in sensation.

Everything goes white for a moment. I can't hear, can't think, can only feel the intensity of my climax as it consumes me completely.

Before I've even fully come down, I feel a cock pressing against my pussy. I'm so swollen, so wet, that he slides in effortlessly. I moan deeply as he fills me, his thick length stretching me perfectly. He groans above me, his breath ragged as he begins to move inside me. The sensation of being so full after such a powerful orgasm is almost too much, but I want more. I need more.

Another cock presses against my lips, and I eagerly open my mouth to take him in. The man beside me holds my head in place as he begins to fuck my mouth. The sensation of two men inside me—one filling my pussy, the other thrusting into my mouth—is pure, unadulterated ecstasy. I've never felt so completely owned, so utterly taken.

I lose myself in the rhythm of their bodies, in the way they use me, their moans mingling with mine, the wet sounds of sex filling the room. It's raw, animalistic, and I love every second of it.

The man in my mouth groans, his cock pulsing as he reaches his climax. He cums hard, filling my mouth with his hot, salty release. I swallow as much as I can, the rest dripping down my chin, messy and perfect. He withdraws, kissing me gently, grinning at the mess he's left behind.

The man inside me is close, his thrusts becoming more erratic, more desperate. He pulls out at the last second, cumming all over my belly and tits, his hot seed coating my skin. I gasp, loving the feeling of being so thoroughly used.

They both leave me, still tied to the bed, still blindfolded, my body trembling with aftershocks. I lay there, panting, my heart racing, knowing more are still to come. My mind is a haze of pleasure, my body raw and sensitive. I've never felt so free, so utterly consumed by lust.

The soft creak of the door and the heavy steps approaching the bed send another shiver of anticipation through me. Whoever it is, I'm ready for him. I've lost all sense of time—minutes and hours blur together in the haze of desire. My body hums with a mixture of exhaustion and arousal, raw and sensitive, yet still craving more. I want more.

I feel the mattress dip under his weight as he sits beside me. For a moment, there's only silence, his presence lingering over me like a shadow. Then, without warning, his hand trails down my body, tracing slow, deliberate lines over my skin, as if he's taking his time to explore every curve, every dip. His touch is confident, teasing. He knows exactly what he's doing.

He leans down, his breath hot against my ear. "You're beautiful like this," he murmurs, his voice deep and familiar, making my heart race. "So open, so ready… just for us."

His words send a thrill through me, and I arch my back in response, desperate for more of his touch.

He chuckles softly, a sound full of dark promise, and shifts his weight, positioning himself between my legs. I can feel him there, close, his cock teasing the entrance of my pussy, hovering just out of reach, the anticipation driving me wild.

I whimper, my body aching for him to take me. To fill me.

"Patience," he whispers, his voice low and commanding. "You've been good, but I want to savor this."

He moves slowly, torturously, guiding his cock to the entrance of my dripping pussy. Inch by inch, he pushes inside, his girth stretching me open. I moan loudly, my back arching off the bed, the sensation of him filling me completely overwhelming. He holds himself there, deep inside me, not moving, just letting me feel how full I am, how completely he possesses me.

"God, you're so tight," he groans, his voice thick with lust. "So fucking perfect."

He begins to move then, slow, powerful thrusts that make my entire body tremble. Each stroke sends a fresh wave of pleasure coursing through me, pushing me closer to the edge once again. My hips move instinctively, rising to meet his every thrust, desperate for more.

But he controls the pace, drawing it out, making me feel every inch of him as he slides in and out, slow and steady. His hands grip my hips, holding me in place, keeping me exactly where he wants me. I'm at his mercy, and I love it.

I can feel the tension building again, the pleasure coiling tight in my belly, threatening to spill over. I'm close, so close, my entire body trembling with need.

"Please," I gasp, my voice barely a whisper. "Please, I need to cum…"

His hand snakes down between my legs, finding my clit, and he begins to rub in slow, deliberate circles. The sensation is overwhelming, and I cry out, my body convulsing with the intensity of it.

"Not yet," he growls, his voice dark and commanding. "Hold on for me. Just a little longer."

I whimper, every nerve in my body on fire, but I try to obey, try to hold back the orgasm that's building inside me. His fingers continue their torturous dance over my clit, teasing, pushing me closer and closer to the edge until I can't take it anymore.

"Please!" I beg, my voice trembling. "Please, let me cum!"

He thrusts harder, faster now, his control slipping as he gets closer to his own release. His fingers on my clit move faster, more insistent, pushing me right to the brink.

And then, with one final, powerful thrust, he lets go. I feel him explode inside me, his cock pulsing, filling me with his hot release. At the same time, my body shatters, the orgasm crashing over me like a tidal wave, so intense it leaves me gasping for air. I scream, my whole body trembling, convulsing, as the pleasure consumes me completely.

For a long moment, there's nothing but pure, raw sensation, the world around me fading away as I ride out the waves of ecstasy. His body collapses on top of mine, heavy and warm, his breath ragged in my ear. I can feel the last pulses of his release inside me, his cock still twitching as we both come down from the high.

He pulls out slowly, gently, leaving me empty and aching. I feel the warmth of his cum trickle down my thighs, mixing with the mess of fluids already coating my skin. My body is a wreck, thoroughly used, thoroughly satisfied.

I lie there, panting, my heart racing, my mind still swimming in the afterglow. I don't know how many men have come through that door tonight, but I've lost count. It doesn't matter. Before it had felt a bit like they were doing a service for me, pushing all my buttons, turning me on and working together to make me cum so hard it felt like my brain was melting. Now it is all about them and their needs. I am purely free-use for them and it makes me feel submissive on a level I have never known. I can hear their happy voices from downstairs and it is such a delicious feeling to lay here tied up and spread open like a living fuckdoll. An object, yes, but an object of desire. I've wanted this, needed this, and now that it's happening, it's even more perfect than I imagined.

Eventually, exhaustion kicks in. My jaw hurts. I am covered in cum and thoroughly sore in every intimate place. I begin to doze off between visitors. As I catch my breath, the door opens again. I tense, waiting for the next man to claim me. But instead, I hear my partner's voice, soft and gentle.

"It's time to rest," he says, coming to sit beside me on the bed. He unbuckles my restraints, freeing my wrists and ankles, and pulls the blindfold from my eyes. The room swims back into focus, dimly lit, the smell of sex heavy in the air.

I blink up at him, my body exhausted but my heart full. He smiles down at me, brushing a strand of hair from my face. "You were incredible tonight," he whispers, his voice full of pride and affection.

I melt into his arms as he pulls me close, wrapping me in his warmth. He kisses the top of my head, his hands soothing over my sore, aching body. We lie there in comfortable silence for a long moment, the world around us falling away as we bask in the afterglow of what we've just shared.

Finally, he helps me up, guiding me into the shower, where he gently washes me clean, his touch tender and loving. I lean into him, letting the warm water wash away the sweat and the cum, the remnants of my wildest fantasy now a sweet memory.

When we're done, I slip into a soft robe, and we head downstairs, where the others are gathered, relaxed and content. The air is filled with laughter and easy conversation, a stark contrast to the intensity of what we've just experienced. I feel a strange sense of shyness as they greet me, but it passes quickly as they shower me with compliments, each of them taking a moment to thank me for the night.

My partner lifts his glass in a toast, his eyes gleaming with mischief. "To an unforgettable night," he says, grinning. Then, with a wicked glint in his eye, he adds, "And wait until you hear what we've got planned for tomorrow."

Another shiver of excitement runs through my body. Tomorrow.

WRESTLING WITH DESIRE

BY PAUL GIBBON

Keywords: WLW, Sapphic, wrestling, restraint, grappling, power play, submission- dominance, forced orgasm, humour, cute, bratty, self-discovery.

Synopsis: Lyra and her girlfriend, Penny, find themselves caught up in an unexpected wrestling match that turns into a playful and erotic contest of strength and control. As Penny reveals her past as a wrestler, the competition heats up, with Lyra initially confident but quickly finding herself overpowered by Penny's skill and strength. Despite Lyra's attempts to fight back and assert herself, she becomes captivated by the sensation of being dominated, discovering a new thrill in being rendered helpless in Penny's grasp. Penny, meanwhile, enjoys unleashing her strength in a way she's never allowed herself to before, leading both women to explore the boundaries of power, submission, and mutual desire in a night that deepens their connection and leaves them eager for more.

WRESTLING WITH DESIRE

"Hey, Penny, are you ready—"

I duck back as my girlfriend's fist sweeps past my nose.

"Whoa!"

Penny makes a comical 'whoops!' expression. "Oh—sorry, Lyra. Didn't see you there—" she begins, but quickly gets distracted by the TV again. Looking at what she was watching, it suddenly makes more sense.

"Come on, don't go for strikes, he's got that scouted! Oh yeah, you left yourself wide open for a takedown, don't look so surprised. And—oh yeah! He got a submission, of course, he did. Jeez!" she says with a roll of her eyes.

I watch her, trying to keep a smile off my face as she mimics the punches and kicks of the two brawny guys in the MMA ring, not performing well enough for her standards. My girlfriend is normally quite reserved, but it's always fun to see her getting enthusiastic like this.

"Yeah, you do remember we had a date tonight?" I ask. "I mean, the match looks really thrilling, but..."

"Huh? Yeah," says Penny, turning off the TV with an embarrassed laugh. "I just get really into it. I was on the wrestling team at university, you know. Won a few trophies!"

"For real?" I knew she was into fitness, but this is new. "So...you're pretty good, huh?"

"Well, I don't like to brag, but—"

"Nah, brag all you like," I say, looking at Penny. There's a good four inches in height between us, even with the volume of my curly hair, and she's not scrawny either. With her cropped blonde hair, muscles, and tattoos, I like to call her my "Amazon princess." It's true, and it always gets her so delightfully flustered.

"Or—even better! Show me?"

"Show you?"

"Yeah! Try some of those moves on me if you're that good—"

"I don't know, Lyra. I don't want to hurt you."

"It'll be fine! I trust you. Unless...oh, I know what it is. You're worried I'll beat you?"

Penny closes her eyes for a moment, visibly trying to fight down a smile. "Lyra, you're not going to beat me."

"Penny, I grew up with three older brothers. I was a terror in the playground too. I know how to fight. Come on!"

"Lyra—"

I make some chicken noises. No, I'm not proud.

Penny rolls her eyes. "All right, fine, fine! We'll wrestle! But some ground rules, okay? First, if it gets uncomfortable, you need to either tap my arm quickly or just say you quit."

"Funny, I was just about to say the same to you."

"And second, get your dress off." She gestures to the floaty sundress I'm wearing. A while back, Penny said she liked that color, that it looked so cute on me, and I saw what she meant—something about yellow on my brown skin just works. Since then, I've never gone on a date with her without something in that color.

"It looks great on you, and I don't want to damage it," she adds, pushing her jeans down and peeling off her t-shirt. Her underwear is sensible and practical—but with an athletic, toned body like hers, even the fanciest of lingerie would not be the main event. I drop my dress in turn, revealing a bra and panties that are a bit lacier and girlier. Penny steps into the center of the room and drops into some sort of stance.

"I'll stick to the basics. And...ready? Okay, go!"

I know exactly what I'm going to do. If I drop low and tackle her to the floor, I can pin her down and just sit on her until she submits. It had been pretty reliable in the school playground.

But my grab just catches a lot of thin air, and somehow, Penny's behind me in one fluid motion. While my mind is still completing the word *Huh?*, she's grabbed me from behind. And somehow, my left leg isn't touching the floor anymore.

She tips me forward neatly, half-supporting me as I go down on the carpet with Penny behind me. She's holding my right arm behind my back in a hold that's both gentle and entirely immovable.

"Hey! That wasn't fair!" I squeak, kicking and trying to reach back. But she's got me. Totally and utterly—even if I could grab her with my spare hand,

I can't exert any force from this angle. My girlfriend has me entirely helpless.

And it feels...good, to a degree that's kind of a shock. Not the losing—I'm seething about that. But at the same time, there's something about being so quickly made powerless like this.

"See what I mean?" she asks, sounding almost embarrassed. "You're scrappy, but I'm trained. You okay, Lyra? I wasn't too rough?"

"No..." I reply, feeling a little light-headed. "Definitely not too rough..."

She gets up and helps me to my feet. "Okay, then come on, clothes back on. The movie's gonna start—"

"Best of three?" I ask. The offer just kind of slips out, but I didn't take it back. Everything Penny just said is correct, about her having an edge on me in every way. But I really want to wrestle her.

"Well, we can do, but what's the point?" she asks.

"The point is, you got lucky," I reply, with a pout. "I'll kick your ass next time!"

"Are you serious?"

I try for an intimidating expression, but I think it comes across more as "upset kitten."

"Totally! Come on, don't hold anything back! I want to see all your moves!"

She reaches for my hands and we lock up, intertwining our fingers. She pushes, and I push back, hard as I can.

I do a takedown on her. Which is a fancy way of saying I shove into her while she's off-balance, and end up straddling her as she's on her back on the floor.

"Strong start...from the challenger!" I gasp, already a bit out of breath but feeling the thrill of victory. I've got her hands pinned, I've got her on her back, and that's pretty good, right? "Now, how about you—AH!"

She'd brought her legs up while I was talking, and now she's locked them around my waist, trapping me in a scissors hold. I'm trapped, and I can feel the pressure of her strong thighs, making it a bit hard to breathe even though she's not particularly straining.

There's always been something I've noticed about Penny. She's strong, she's tough, but she's so shy and cautious about using her strength. When she's around me, she almost seems embarrassed in case she accidentally looms over me or intimidates me. She's not bossy in bed either, even though I've told her more than once I wouldn't mind if she was.

This is the first time she's really used her strength on me. And it's really arousing.

"Oh fuck..."

"Is it too much?" she asks.

"No! Definitely not too much!" I reply hastily. "I can get you—oh!"

She repositions her hands and grabs my wrists. And suddenly, I don't feel in control anymore, even if I'm still technically on top.

"It's over, Lyra. Now, I can just squeeze you till you can't breathe, and make you tap that way." says Penny. She's interrupted by an especially furious bout of thrashing, as I try to force her off through sheer brute strength. But I'm not very brutish.

"Jeez, Lyra, take a hint!" she gasps, but she's sounding like she's getting into this as well. "What do I need to do to—you know what? You asked for this!"

She rolls us both over and, trapped in her legs like this, I have to go with her until I'm on my back with her squatting over my waist and our positions reversed. I try and fight it as Penny grabs one of my arms with both her hands and wedges it between my body and her thigh.

"Stay still—be a good girl—"

"Nuh-uh!" I reply, trying to think of what I can do to even the odds. I can feel my left arm being pinned in place, and I expect my right arm to follow it before long, forcing me to admit defeat. I try to think of anything I can do to even the odds, some sort of weak spot that—

"Aha!" I call out as I use my secret technique— grabbing Penny's crotch and rubbing her through her underwear. She really wasn't expecting that, to judge by how she stops dead and gasps, her face flushing almost immediately.

"Lyra—mmm! What are you--?"

"Didn't learn this at wrestling school, did you?" I reply, slipping my hand inside. The angle is a bit awkward, but I can still get a good motion going with my fingers, to either side of that little bump. Penny bites her finger, letting out a cute little groan.

"Hey, no fair! This is fighting dirty!" she protests.

"Better make me stop then..."

With a grunt, I manage to buck her partially off so we end up lying side by side, with my arm still pinned under her body. But before we can start grappling again, Penny holds up her hand.

"Lyra, baby...are you sure that's how you want to play this?"

The concern in her voice catches me off guard. Of course, Penny cares for me, and I know she'd never do anything if she thought I wasn't into it. But there's something else in her tone—a kind of eagerness.

"No holds barred, right?" I tease, my grin widening. "And hey, maybe if this fight gets dirty, then I might actually beat you!"

I dart my hand down toward her crotch again, but she's faster. She grabs my wrist and, slowly and firmly, moves my hand behind my head. Now she's got both my arms pinned with just one of her hands. No matter how much I squirm, I can't free my arms— or stop her from trapping one of my legs between her thighs.

"You can tell me to stop anytime, you know that?" she says gently. I can feel her breath on my cheek as I struggle. She's concerned for me...but there's something else simmering beneath the surface. She wants to cut loose. She wants permission.

And I give it.

"Do your worst!"

Her free hand trails across my belly, slipping under the waistband of my panties. I'm squirming, thrashing, trying to get free. Genuinely trying...but also hoping to fail. And then it clicks, and I realize what I want. Why I was so keen on doing this.

I want to do my best, and fail. I want my girlfriend to overpower me. It's so much more fun than just rolling over and submitting right from the start!

And when her fingers slip in, I realize exactly how much this has been turning me on, as all the pent-up desire suddenly ignites, and I let out a whimpering gasp. I strain, trying to escape. But as I expected (and hoped), she's got me in a position I can't break free from.

I hear Penny take a breath in, about to ask if I'm okay with this, so I pre-empt her.

"What, you're gonna try and make me cum? It's not gonna work, you can't do it!" I challenge, my voice playful, teasing.

I feel like such a brat! And Penny takes the cue, her tone shifting to something more predatory—like a cat that just found a mouse.

"All right. So if I can't make you cum, you've got nothing to worry about... you just lay there... and don't cum for me, okay?"

"Nuh-uh!" I squeak as she curls those fingers inside me, going straight for those spots that make my legs tremble. "Not gonna cum!"

"I know you're not! I'm just wasting my time!" she agrees, punctuating her words by leaning down and kissing me. "You're not getting wet. You're not getting turned on at all! I'm just imagining it!"

"Oh fuck—" I groan as she starts thrusting nice and slow, before remembering I'm meant to be fighting her and straining to break the hold—in vain. I'm genuinely trying to escape, but I'm not expecting to succeed. As a matter of fact, I'm counting on failing. There's something about the paradox of my body fighting to get free, while my pussy is eagerly surrendering, obeying the commands her fingers are giving. Every time I fight back and fail, it sends a rush of submissive excitement shooting straight up my spine.

She starts gradually speeding up her fingers, the slick sounds barely audible over my heavy breathing. As she leans over me, I can see the effort—how her lighter skin is flushing, how her muscles are taut, even how she's deliberately controlling her breathing to conserve her energy better than me.

I can feel the power coming from Penny, the strength she's using on me. And then there's the eager anticipation on her face. I don't think I'm the only one who discovered something new about themselves tonight.

"Oh—oh fuck—not gonna cum—you can't make me—"

She gives an indulgent chuckle. "No, of course I can't. You just lay there and focus on not cumming!"

But I can feel my body yielding to her, reaching the tipping point. My breath catches, and then—it's starting. Despite my best efforts to fight the pleasure, I'm cumming.

"No, not—not—ah! Oh shit, that's so—fuck, Penny! Ah! Cumming!"

"Cumming?" she asks, her voice full of mock concern as she fingers me even faster. "No, that can't be right, you said you weren't cumming! You definitely said that! You want me to stop?"

"No! No! Don't stop! Don't—don't—oh, oh, oh—AH!"

My body jolts, nearly breaking out of her grasp as I cum hard. My mind goes blank as it just overpowers me, one of the most intense orgasms I've ever had. Finally, the tension breaks, and I collapse back, completely limp and exhausted. Penny slowly pulls her slick fingers out as my hips twitch and I pant open-mouthed for air.

And when I'm able to look at her straight and remember which way is down, she runs her fingers down my forehead and nose, leaving a trail of my own juices on my face, before she puts them into my mouth and makes me taste myself.

"Mmm…"

"I win," she says, releasing the hold and stroking my hair. "That was fun!"

"Yeah…" I reply. "So good…"

"Here's a story, Lyra. I realized I was gay when I noticed how much I enjoyed grappling with other women. Overpowering them, making them submit to me. I tried to keep that side of things from ever showing because it didn't feel fair to my opponents if I was just using them to get off. But you just gave me permission to…"

She kisses me, sweet and tender. "Thank you. That was so much fun."

"Let's do it again."

"Yeah…I'd love that. Some other time, we can do it properly—"

I sit up, and start getting my bra off. "I mean now, Penny. Best of five?"

"Best of—" she begins, but then smirks and starts to pull her panties down. "Baby, you sure about this?"

"You just got lucky!" I reply with a pout, as we both get naked. "I've got your number now. You'll be the one cumming all over the carpet!"

"That a fa—oof!"

I grab for her hands, trying to tip her over. But with a momentary glance behind her, Penny somehow reverses that and sends me right into the soft couch. I try to find purchase on the overstuffed upholstery, but that's when I feel Penny's arm going around my neck from behind. I know that's not good.

"You never learn, baby!" she says, and pulls me back, bringing our two naked bodies down to the floor, with me lying on top of her but facing away, controlled by her arm around my neck, which she locks in with her other arm.

She's not choking me. But I can't reach back with any strength, and I can feel the pressure on my throat. It's enough to tell me that if Penny wanted to, she could put me out like a light. In barely five seconds, she's got me helpless, and the mere thought causes another surge of excitement.

"Here's something else about fighting!" she says from behind, nipping at my ear with her teeth. "It's not all about being strong or a scrapper. That helps, but it's all about leverage. Knowing where a body bends, and where it doesn't."

She releases my throat and forces my arm behind my back, sandwiched between our bodies. The other one, she lifts up and forces me to point up. I can't move one arm at all, and the other is held in place by Penny threading her own arm under my armpit and behind my head. It's technically free, but I can't lower it enough to interfere with what she's doing to me.

"That's called a half nelson, by the way," she says, running her free hand down my body as I squirm on top of her. She cups each breast in turn, squeezing them gently and tweaking the nipples. It feels so embarrassing to be so easily manhandled like this, but that embarrassment is just another bit of fuel for the frantic desire I'm feeling right now.

All the while, I'm straining, trying to break free—but once again, she's got me all tied up, locked in place by my own joints. I wasn't ready for how quickly I'd tire out, how my muscles have started aching. But Penny, apart from being flushed, seems completely fresh. Looks like all that time at the gym doing cardio wasn't just to make her look fantastic.

"No! Don't you dare!" I gasp as she begins to trail her hand across my belly, and I clamp my thighs shut.

"There's no point resisting, Lyra," she says. "I'm gonna get that pussy, and I'm gonna make you cum again."

"Nuh-uh!"

"Uh-huh. I know that after you pop once, you're so much more sensitive the second time around. How many seconds do you think you'd last once my fingers are working away in there, Lyra? Ten? Twenty?" She gives a dirty laugh, her earlier nerves entirely gone. "Oh, I don't think so. I think I'd just slip them in, and—OH!"

"You're not getting in—" I begin, but she moves her legs. She hooks her ankles inside mine before I can think to cross my feet, and then she begins to open me up.

I fight it. I fight it as hard as I can. But I'm already exhausted, and it wouldn't be a contest even if I weren't. And that's before you factor in her ability to reach my submissive side, to make me forget I'm meant to be fighting her. When I lose some ground, I don't regain it. And slowly, inexorably, Penny is prying me open until my legs are wide apart and my pussy is exposed and vulnerable.

"Feeling a little weak?" she asks over my shoulder. "Yeah, wrestling is tougher than it looks, isn't it?"

She heaves us both into a sitting position without loosening the holds on my arms or legs. Propped against the couch, Penny makes a show of licking her fingers. She trails them down over my body again. And then—

"Oh FUCK, Penny!"

—she's back in. Immediately finding the same spot she was working last time and beginning to pump. I try to pull away, but I'm almost helpless. And as I watch those fingers start emerging and sinking into me, slick with my wetness, and feel the surges of pleasure shooting through my sensitive body, maybe I don't mind that. Penny's right; I'm always more sensitive the second time around.

I put up some token resistance, as much as I can muster to let Penny know that I'm still technically fighting her and she can't let me go, but I've genuinely got no strength left. All I can do is squirm and writhe as she works my pussy, forcing me toward another orgasm. And just thinking of the power and control contained in that word *forcing* makes me go weak, makes me crave her touch and the way she's handling me.

She's going harder, rapid liquid sounds accompanying her fingers. And to make it better—or worse—she's kissing my neck too! I'm under attack from all sides, and—

"Penny! Ah!"

"It's not too much, is it?" she asks. "Just cum, baby girl."

"Make me!"

"Oh, I don't have to make you!" she replies, biting my ear. "This is a good, obedient pussy. It wants to cum, not fight. So just give in. Just cum for me, Lyra, I can feel how much you want to!"

She punctuates that with a nice deep thrust that makes my eyes roll up for a moment. It's almost too much to bear, and almost at the point where the overstimulation would become painful, but the important word there is "almost."

"Fuck...Penny. You're gonna break my pussy! Ah! Don't stop!"

I hear a sharp gasp from behind me and feel her arms and legs tense where she's restraining me as we're sat up together, and I guess I just triggered something in her.

"You can take it! Cum for me, Lyra. Give in to it, give in to me, give in, just—ah yes! There you go!"

There I go indeed. I scream as I feel the climax take hold, shaking atop Penny. I'm helpless, and my girlfriend is forcing me to cum all over her hand—and thinking about it like that makes it even more intense—and she doesn't slow down. Immediately afterward, I can feel another orgasm building—

"Penny, gonna cum—again—"

"It's all right. Who said you just had to cum once? You can cum as many times as you like!"

And so I do. I cum once again, helplessly pinned by my girlfriend. I feel something loosen within me, and I moan as I squirt across the floor, my body shaking until I'm entirely limp and drained. It feels like she's entirely broken me, and I'm quite happy with that.

Finally, she lets me go. As I'm slumped there, she picks me up—just casually picks me up in a romantic bridal carry—and lays me on the sofa to recover. And as I finally get my breath back and the overstimulation ebbs at last, she holds up a hand.

"No, Lyra. We're not doing best of seven. I don't think you'd survive!"

"Aww!" I say with mock annoyance. "But we are doing this again, right?"

She gives a nervous laugh. "Do you really... like losing to me?"

"...maybe I do? Yeah, definitely!" I reply, with a cheeky grin. "You were so hot, just letting go and controlling me. You're really sexy when you're not scared to use your strength! But I'd still like to kick your ass fair and square... one day. So teach me a bit about wrestling?"

"It's a deal!" says my girlfriend, sealing it with a kiss on my forehead. I giggle and then remember something.

"Oh! Penny, haven't you forgotten something?"

"Hmm?"

I lay back on the couch, and, with a tug on her hand, invite Penny to come up and sit on my face.

"The winner should claim her prize, right?"

And she does.

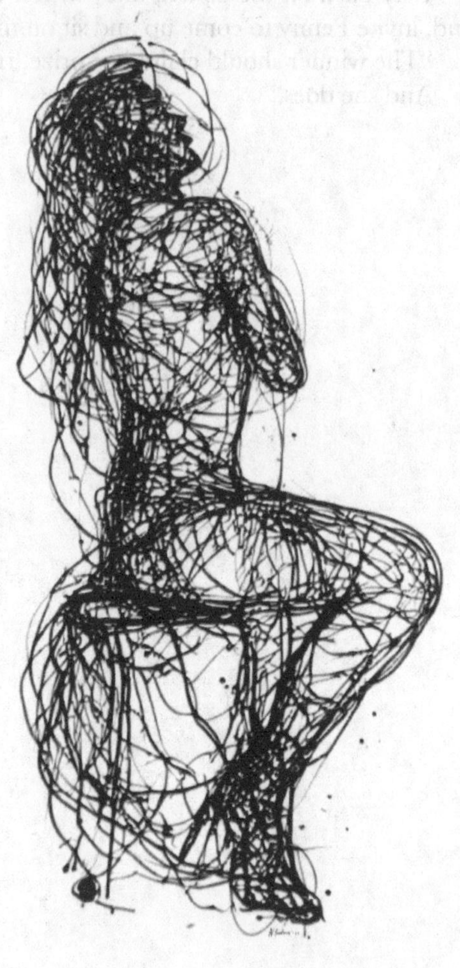

AN ARTIST'S MUSE

BY TIGGS

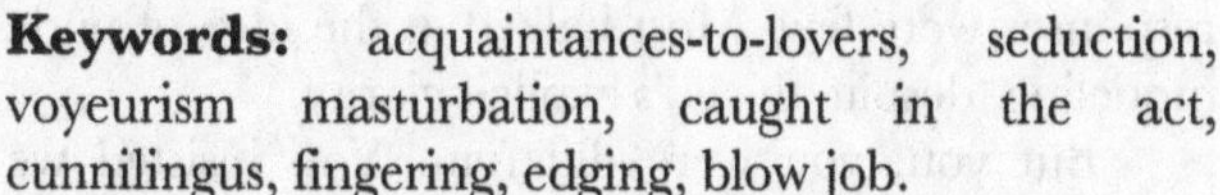

Keywords: acquaintances-to-lovers, seduction, voyeurism masturbation, caught in the act, cunnilingus, fingering, edging, blow job.

Synopsis: A struggling artist finds himself captivated by a mysterious new model whose quiet confidence and sensual allure awaken desires he never anticipated. From the first session, an intense, unspoken tension simmers between them, with her teasing glances and subtle touches driving him to the edge of self-control. As the boundaries between art and obsession blur, their sessions become an electrifying dance of temptation and seduction, leading to a climactic night where fantasies are unleashed, and both artist and muse find themselves caught in the throes of a passion that defies all restraint.

AN ARTIST'S MUSE

Finding a new model is always a challenge. Hannah had been perfect—professional, reliable—but she finished graduate school and moved across the country. I placed an ad in the campus paper, but the responses were few. Most balked at the idea of nude modeling, despite the ad's explicit clarity.

But you, you were different. You insisted we didn't need to meet in person first. On the phone, you mentioned you knew Hannah and had spoken to her, that you understood what was involved. I figured, why not? I had nothing to lose. We agreed on a time, and I hung up.

You arrived early for our first session, catching me slightly off guard. I was still in the studio, finishing a piece when I heard the doorbell. I scrambled to clean the paint from my hands, trying to look somewhat presentable before I answered.

Your back was to me as you began to walk away. I called out, and you spun around to face me. Your expression was unreadable—annoyed or relieved, perhaps both—but your piercing eyes bored right through me. I greeted you awkwardly, extending my paint-covered hand, which you glanced at with a mix of amusement and disdain. I quickly withdrew it, apologized, and gestured for you to come inside.

You moved with a grace and confidence that few possess, though a flicker of shyness danced in your eyes. It intrigued me immediately. I led you to the studio, where natural light flooded the space through the glass walls and ceiling. You set your bag on the chaise, politely declining my offer of a drink, seeming eager to get down to business.

I tried to ease the tension, asking about school, your interests, but you gave only brief, distracted replies, your eyes wandering around the studio. I asked why you wanted to do nude modeling, and you seemed flustered, nervously tucking your hair behind your ear, mumbling something about grad school expenses. You asked if there was a place to undress, and I directed you to a room just outside the studio, mentioning a robe was there for you.

Minutes later, you returned, clutching the robe closed. I directed you to the chaise, explaining I'd like to start with some sketches, my usual practice with new models, to help us both feel more comfortable. With your back to me, you let the robe slip off your shoulders, glancing over with those big, inquisitive eyes. I couldn't help but get lost in them.

You turned slowly, letting the robe drop to the floor, but you kept your gaze away, fixing on something outside in the garden. I, however, was captivated by you. My eyes followed the line of your jaw, down your neck, to the delicate curve of your clavicle. I noticed your breath had deepened, making your beautiful breasts rise and fall slightly. My gaze lingered on them, and I couldn't help but memorize their shape, the way your nipples had hardened—not from cold, I thought, but something else.

I continued down to your hips, your thighs, where your hands rested. I imagined them as mine, caressing you from behind. I cleared my throat, shaking off the daydream, and began to sketch.

You were shy at first, unsure of yourself, but with a little direction, you relaxed. You chose poses that beautifully accentuated your features, instinctively finding the best light. I became engrossed in drawing your curves, the play of light on your skin.

After a while, we took a break. This time, you accepted my offer of tea. As we stood in the kitchen, you were so close I could smell your shampoo or perfume—intoxicating, drawing me in. When the kettle boiled, we both reached for it, your fingers grazing mine, sending a jolt through me. You pulled back quickly, and I poured the water, trying to steady myself.

We chatted lightly, but I was distracted by the way you stared at me, biting your lip, your hand tucked inside your robe. The soft "uh-huhs" and "yeahs" you offered as I spoke sounded almost like moans, unsettling me. We returned to the studio to continue.

Your demeanor had changed; confidence replaced your earlier shyness. You were almost flirty, choosing poses that felt daring, staring at me as if daring me not to look away. I was entranced.

When you slipped back into your robe to change, you came over to examine the sketches, seeming pleased. I handed you a key to the studio in case I was ever late for a session, and your fee. You leaned in unexpectedly, hugging me, pressing your body against mine. The scent of you filled my senses, and I lost myself for a moment until you pulled away.

We had several more sessions like this, each one charged with tension. You took every opportunity to touch me—brushing my arm, placing your hand on my back, or bending over to retrieve your robe, showing me glimpses of your body. I wanted to dismiss it as playful teasing, but I couldn't stop thinking about you.

I booked an evening session, needing the moodier lighting for the piece I had in mind. You were to arrive at 8:30 p.m.; I had a client meeting earlier that evening. As I left the garage, I noticed a faint light from the studio. I was certain I had turned off all the lights before leaving.

Approaching, I saw you inside, and I stopped dead. Candles were lit all around, casting an otherworldly glow. You lay on the chaise, robe open, one leg on the floor, the other bent, spreading yourself wide. One hand teased your nipple, the other between your legs, fingers spreading your lips, your pussy glistening in the soft light.

I watched, my breath quickening, feeling myself harden against my pants. You plunged your finger into yourself, and I shifted, adjusting to ease the pressure. I hesitated—should I stay or leave? But I couldn't move; I was mesmerized by the sight of you pleasuring yourself, your quiet moans filtering through the thin glass.

Your sounds grew louder, and I found myself stepping closer, entering the house quietly. Your scent filled the air as I neared. Lost in your own pleasure, you didn't notice me until I stood right in front of you, watching your fingers work your dripping wet pussy.

When you opened your eyes, you didn't stop as I thought you might. Instead, you turned toward me, biting your lip, continuing to pleasure yourself, your gaze fierce but sultry, drawing me in.

I hesitated, stroking myself through my pants, torn between watching and acting. But then, your lips parted, and in a breathless voice, you pleaded,

"Fuck me, please fuck me! I need you."

Shocked, but eager, I dropped to my knees and replaced your hand with my mouth. Your slick heat covered my face as I slowly licked and sucked at your clit, savoring every moment as you squirmed and moaned above me. Your hips bucked, but I held you down, making you beg for release.

Your soft "please" wasn't enough. I paused, teasing, urging you to say more. Your eyes pleaded, but I demanded, coaxing out your deepest desires. Finally, you confessed—how much you wanted me, how you'd fantasized about this since our first session.

I edged you relentlessly, driving you to the brink again and again before finally allowing you to cum, your body shuddering around my fingers. You collapsed in front of me, breathless. When you recovered, you leaned in, your lips brushing mine, teasing with a light kiss before you pulled back.

I couldn't resist any longer. I cupped your face, kissing you deeply. Your moans filled the space between us as I kissed down your neck, feeling the goosebumps rise beneath my touch. You responded eagerly, pulling at my clothes, exposing my skin to yours.

You took control, guiding me to the chaise, your mouth teasing down my body until your lips found my cock. You began slowly, eyes locked on mine, taking me deeper, your mouth hot and wet. The sight and sounds of you were almost enough to make me lose control.

But I stopped you, wanting more. You climbed onto my lap, straddling me, your body warm and slick against mine. With a sly smile, you guided me inside you, gasping as I filled you completely. I held your hips, feeling your every movement, lost in the rhythm you set.

You rode me with growing intensity, your eyes never leaving mine, until you came with a cry, your body quivering. I held you close, whispering praise, kissing your neck as you caught your breath.

But we weren't done. I lifted you, moved you, laid you down, my cock still buried deep inside you. I thrust into you harder, driven by the look in your eyes, your urgent whispers, "Please, cum inside me."

Your pleas pushed me over the edge. I came hard, deep inside you, collapsing against your back, both of us breathless and spent. As we lay there, tangled together, you asked what I was thinking.

I chuckled, "Not quite how I expected tonight's session to go."

You smiled, turning to face me, "Oh, it's exactly how I planned it."

RECONCILIATION

BY DANTE REMY

Keywords: sinners-to-lovers, stranger fantasy, hook up, slow burn, nipple play, clit play, g-spot orgasm, sin, confessional mutual orgasm.

Synopsis: A lonely woman returning to her hometown finds unexpected connection through a dating app, leading to a night of intense emotional and erotic intimacy with a stranger—only to discover days later that he is the priest hearing her confession. What begins as an attempt to absolve her guilt transforms into a mutual reckoning, as both confront the raw truth of their desires and the unbearable pull between sacred duty and carnal need. Their shared confessional becomes a crucible of lust and redemption, blurring the line between sin and salvation, and culminating in a defiant, sensual act of spiritual union. In the flickering shadows of the church, they find not only forgiveness—but a love that dares to reclaim both the flesh and the soul.

RECONCILIATION

As I push open the heavy door of the confessional booth and step inside, the familiar scent of polished wood and old incense wraps around me, thick with the musk of old prayers. The small window screen slides open with a faint creak, revealing the shadowed outline of the priest on the other side, a silhouette of absolution waiting to hear my sin.

"Bless me, Father, for I have sinned. It's been…uh…two years since my last confession," I admit, a little awkwardly, shifting slightly on the velvet-lined seat, my voice barely more than a breath against the quietude that enfolds me. The air inside the booth feels thick, heavy with the burden of unspoken confessions and my heart flutters with a blend of trepidation and release.

"Yes, Father…it's been a while," I continue, responding to his unspoken question. There's a certain comfort in anonymity, the face obscured behind the screen, listening without judgment. "Well, I'm a parishioner…I mean, my family is. I've been away and moved home recently…job hunting…just getting my life in order…" I trail off, trying to gather my thoughts, to arrange them into coherent sentences. It's harder than I expected, laying bare the chaos of my life to a near stranger, even one sworn to secrecy.

My confession starts to pour out, a mix of relief and reluctance tangling my words. "I just... I met someone, but I feel such guilt," I confess, the words heavy with an emotion I hadn't fully acknowledged until now.

"Why? Well, it's how and, uhm…how it all turned out…" I hesitate, not sure how to explain the twisted knot of feelings inside me. The silence from the other side of the screen is patient, expectant.

I take a deep breath. "It's just that…all of my friends have moved away…I just wanted to meet someone…so, I joined GetSome…it's a hook-up app…" The admission feels trivial, silly even, when spoken out loud, but the priest's response is understanding, unphased by the modernity of my sin.

"Oh, you know what it is… Yeah, I'm sure you hear a lot about these sorts of things in confession…" His acknowledgment is a small comfort, and it emboldens me to continue.

"So, maybe out of boredom, or just wanting to, uhm… personally and physically connect with someone, I responded to a match," I admit, a nervous laugh escaping me. The priest's presence, unseen but felt, encourages me to reveal more, to delve deeper into my transgression.

I recount how it all started innocently enough— a notification, a chat that stretched through an afternoon. "He was a lot like me, Father… professional…in a new city…looking to connect with someone…" The words tumble out, a confession of loneliness as much as any sin.

"We connected over so much, laughed, shared stories… I hadn't really opened up like this to someone in a long time," I explain, the warmth of the memory suffusing the cold space around me.

The day we met up was perfect, sunny and breezy. "He complimented me on my sundress," I recall, the memory vivid, etched deeply in my mind. We didn't go to his place or mine. Instead, we went to a museum, walking the halls, lost in conversation, in each other's company. "It felt like we knew each other, like fast friends," I reminisce, a smile in my voice despite the guilt.

We sat in front of a large impressionist painting, making up stories about its origins, each tale more fanciful than the last. The afternoon slipped away without either of us noticing, wrapped up in the bubble of our newfound connection. Eventually, we moved to a hotel terrace, a decision made in the reluctance to part ways.

As the evening grew dark, my desires shifted, deepened. "I suggested we get a room," I confess, the weight of the decision pressing down on me even now. "Nothing had to happen, but…" The words trail off as I remember the intimacy that followed, my sundress falling to the floor, his eyes on me, filled with a longing that mirrored my own.

The silence on the other side of the screen is unbearable. "It was my idea…to get the room," I say suddenly, "he was even hesitant." I feel my face begin to burn red from shame, embarrassment, and…desire over what transpired. The priest assures me that in these situations, both man and woman are acting on true feelings, that wanting someone is not sin in and of itself.

"Oh Father, I put up no resistance when he touched me." This brings a rustle of unease, so I think, from the priest, yet kind words follow. He suggests I share what happened next to express my true feelings through reconciliation. I agree. I bare all.

"When we entered the room, I let my sundress fall to the floor and waited for him to take me." I spoke in a soft, meticulous, pattern. In a rash decision, I hadn't worn a bra and I stood in just my panties and two-inch sandals, watching the city lights stream through the dark room. My nipples were erect. My panties, stained with wetness. He approached me without a word, lips caressing my neck, hands cupping my breasts, teasing my nipples.

"Father?" I breathe out, caught in the passion of my words, determined to speak every detail to my anonymous confidant. Perhaps he is uncomfortable with my honesty, as a sign and rustle fill the air. I kept my desire bottled up inside for too long. He would hear everything and, then, judge me for my sins.

"I turned to him and we kissed for the first time, our tongues exploring…our hands pulling each other closer." His kisses trailed down my neck, to my nipples, as he turned me again and explored my wetness with a finger. Teasing one nipple, kissing my neck, two fingers now entered me, curling up slightly, hitting a center of pleasure so deep that I moaned. "Oh, Father, I wanted him so badly, his fingers slid into me without resistance, touching me deeply, and then trailed out slowly to my clit, circling it, teasing, as he pinched harder on my nipple."

"Father, shall I go on? I'm sorry…I need to tell you…" I clench my dress into a fist, feeling flames of want overtaking me. The priest tells me to continue, to describe the path of my passion. "Thank you, Father."

"I could feel his cock, straining against his pants, hard against my ass." I recall in a desperate whisper. I wanted him inside me, but he was bringing me to orgasms too easily to resist. I arched my hips, each time his fingers plunged into me, soaked with my wetness, curling deep inside me, moans of ecstasy escaping me,, and then slowly out and circling my clit. I grasped his hips, pressing his pulsing cock onto. It felt as if it would explode. I was cumming and I wanted him to feel my body overtaken by the pleasure he was giving me. His fingertips circled my clit relentlessly, as orgasm washed over me. I held my breath between waves of pleasure, not ready to let go of him, and, then, gasped as two fingers entered me deeply again, touching the depths of my desire, stroking slowly, beckoning my orgasm back from reprieve. My legs began to shake. I would have fallen had he not held me tighter in his arms. The room began to spin. My pussy tightened around his fingers, cumming in contractions that overtook me, once again. In this moment, I lived only for this fulfilling euphoria.

His arms wrapped around my body as I struggled to recover, shaking and breathing in starts. His wet hand traced up my body, and I took his fingers into my mouth, tasting of sweet delight. His breath against my neck was comforting. He held me for what seemed an eternity, the lights of the city shadowing my glowing body.

Perhaps it was no accident that I wore the same sundress to the confessional today, because I found myself aroused, as if reliving these very moments of passion. My hand had instinctively lifted my dress above my thigh, slid under my panties, and comforted my wet desire. My breathing had become heavy and was joined by sighs from the priest, who clearly was at odds with the details I retold.

Pulling my dress over my thigh, I continue, "I felt so wanted by him, Father. How could this not have been right?" I asked, implying what happened next. The priest responded quietly, assuring me that my truth was not to be judged. Knowingly, he asked what my lover related to me.

"He turned me around and kissed me. Then, held my arms and took a step back. A serious look crossed his face for the first time." I grow silent, pondering his words. I had just confessed my lust. Now, I will bare my soul.

"He said that giving me pleasure was enough to make him happy. He was destined for a life lived for others and that he had given himself to someone else." I sigh, "He said what we had done was beautiful. That, I was beautiful in every way." I think about my next words. "He told me he would never forget me, this moment, and that he would travel far away."

A tear trickles down my burning cheek. "Father, I feel like I ruined a part of him..that I…I was so selfish to take pleasure from him. It was all too fast. Too fast to know how I could be my best self for him."

The priest hesitates on my words, then speaks to my heart.

"You think I was my best self? But, how…how, Father?" I ask, leaning into the screen.

He speaks to me, in a familiar way.

"I gave myself over to him? We…we both gave something of ourselves…to each other? Yes, Father, I can see how that can be a beautiful thing, but what about…"

The rustling and movement on the other side of the partition jolts me. I hears the priest's confession door open, and then close, after some hesitation.

"Father, are you, who are you?"

Concerned, I stand up quickly and escape my confinement. Finding the priest's door ajar, I open it without thinking and find him looking up at me from his chair with needy eyes, his cock glistening with want in his hand. This beautiful man, unable to contain his desire for me. Not just any priest, but him—the man from the terrace, the museum, the hotel room. Our reunion is unexpected, intense, filled with emotions neither of us can fully articulate.

I hold his head in my hands, kissing him, needing him. He confesses too—his own sins, his own desires, his own doubts about his path. A sacred promise to himself that he would never leave me again, if God would allow us to find each other. And in that confession, a new understanding is revealed, a new beginning.

"I'm glad it happened… I still want you…I want you more than ever," I whisper, my words a mirror of his own.

As before, I let my sundress fall to the ground, stepping out of my panties, while his hands caress my body. Our final act, a blend of sin and salvation, takes place not in the sanctity of the church, but in the seclusion of the confessional, the line between sacred and profane blurred beyond recognition.

His cock pulses for me, pent up by my words, ready to be released. I straddle him and slowly lower myself onto his cock, watching his face turn from despair to bliss, taking him deep inside me. My hands ran through his hair, pulling his heads back, as I begin fucking him, lifting myself and slowly returning to hungrily take all of his need. His hands fall to the sides, giving himself completely over to me, bucking his hips gently to ensure I take every inch of him. We breathe moans, joining the chorus of prayers that have for centuries asked for God's forgiveness. Ours are blessed by a bond of lust that transcends good and evil.

His breathing grows more desperate, as does mine, and I quicken my pace, fucking his cock harder to bring me to orgasm with his. I feel his cock stiffen and pulse, as he prepares to give me his life. Bringing his head into my breasts, and holding him tight, smothering his long moans of orgasm, holding him hard, taking him. His gives me every drop of his cum. We orgasm in matching contractions of pleasure, only catching our breath when we are assured every final wave of ecstasy has passed through our bodies. Kissing, smiling, laughing in delight, we gather ourselves and make plans to reunite and to live as one.

As we leave the confessional, our future uncertain yet filled with a shared longing, I realize reconciliation comes in many forms. And sometimes, it's not just about confessing sins, but about embracing the complexities of human connections, however imperfect they may be. We light a candle at the altar, hand-in-hand, as he recites Matthew 5:24: "Leave your gift there in front of the altar. First go and be reconciled to them; then come and offer your gift." Together we find not just absolution in each other's arms, but a profound reconciliation of souls, united and emboldened by the strength of a love that defies convention.

CASUAL ENCOUNTERS

BY ARTGASIM

Keywords: Female POV, MFM, Stranger, Fsub, Blindfold, Cunnilingus, Blow Jobs, Handjobs, Spit Roast, ThroatPie, SubSpace, Aftercare.

Synopsis: A woman confesses her desire for an MFM fantasy to her dominant partner, who eagerly arranges an encounter where she is blindfolded and pleasured by both him and a mysterious stranger. As she navigates the intense sensations of being touched, teased, and filled at both ends, the anonymity and erotic tension heighten her arousal. Under her dom's guidance, she finds herself on her knees, caught in a carnal dance of submission and pleasure, climaxing in a mix of lust, mystery, and satisfaction, all while wondering who the stranger was, savoring the thrill of the unknown long after the experience ends.

CASUAL ENCOUNTERS

"What's on your horny mind?" he asks, a teasing glint in his eye. He knows me too well, sensing the shift in my thoughts.

"I'd like to explore an MFM," I whisper softly, my tone filled with a mix of anticipation and nervous excitement. "You, me, and Mr. Whoever. You take the lead, of course, and facilitate the encounter," I continue, feeling my heartbeat quicken. "I'm yours, and he's our extra," I finish, my cheeks flushed with both shyness and desire.

"As it should be," he replies, a sly smile spreading across his face. I can see the gears in his mind already turning, plotting the possibilities, envisioning every moment.

❦

When our planned date night arrives, we meet in the hotel room, just like we always do. There's something so deliciously familiar yet thrillingly new in these moments. We take our time, savoring each touch, each kiss, every whispered promise of what's to come. I love the way he teases me, taking his time with foreplay, his fingers grazing my skin, lighting fires wherever they land.

And then, with a swift motion, the blindfold goes on.

He loves to play with me like this, heightening every sensation. The feel of his hands on my body—

pinching, squeezing, rubbing, fingering me—drives me mad. He always lets me touch him, lets me stroke his hard length, but never too much, never enough to quench the need he's kindled inside me. He just wants me desperate, aching, on the edge.

And then I sense it—the moment everything changes. I feel the shift in the air, the tension that tells me we are no longer alone.

He begins by sitting on my chest, guiding his cock to my mouth. I suck eagerly, lost in the sensation, when I feel hands spreading my legs, a tongue flicking against my wet, swollen lips.

For a second, I think it might just be his hands—until I feel a third hand…and then a fourth. I try to gasp, my mouth stuffed with his cock, but all that escapes is a moan.

His chuckle reverberates through me, vibrating against my lips. I'm surprised but not resistant. The thrill of a mystery tongue lapping at my pussy, fingers teasing me, heightens my arousal. He's done it—he's made our fantasy a reality.

"Just enjoy yourself," he whispers, his voice calm and steady, a comforting anchor in the storm of sensations.

I hear him gripping the headboard for balance, growling in pleasure as he thrusts slowly into my mouth. He loves to watch me, to see how I react as I grind my wet pussy against the stranger's mouth, my body moving on its own, desperate for more.

He directs a shift in position, and I feel the bed dip as both men move to kneel on either side of my head. Their hands are everywhere, touching, stroking, exploring. I feel my clit throb as wet fingers slide in and out of me, my senses overloaded, unable to distinguish who is who.

A cock presses against my lips, and I open wide, taking it in, feeling the slow, girthy thrust. The blindfold heightens everything—every touch, every sensation. It's all I have to focus on, and I'm overwhelmed, lost in the feeling.

My hands roam, tracing the lines of muscles, groping firm asses, exploring every inch of whoever this is. My mouth alternates between the two cocks, tasting, sucking, savoring them both. My pussy is drenched, my body trembling with need.

He loves to tease me, making me wait. "Can you handle the wait?" he always asks, his voice taunting.

My noises betray me—whimpers, moans, gasps, my body pleading for more.

He decides it's time. "Get off the bed," he orders. I feel his hand on my arm, guiding me down to my knees. "It doesn't matter which way you face," he says with a grin. "You're getting filled at both ends."

I feel a rush of wetness down my thighs as I position myself on all fours, my ass up, my pussy slick and ready. My mouth opens, tongue slightly out, waiting for whatever comes next.

I feel the tip of a cock against my lips, and I take it in deep, feeling his hand on my head, guiding me. Then, the other cock pushes into my pussy from behind, filling me with a deep, satisfying stretch. Fingers dig into my hips, pulling me onto him, driving his cock deeper into me.

The rhythm is slow but deep, deliberate. Each thrust makes my body jolt, my ass stinging from an occasional slap. I love the way they both use me, one cock in my mouth, another in my cunt, every thrust sending ripples of pleasure through my body.

He groans behind me, a sound of approval. I know that voice—it's him. My beacon in the dark. He tells the stranger he'll love it when it's his turn.

The stranger has been so quiet—just heavy breathing and the occasional grunt. The unknown drives me crazy, adds to the thrill.

Then I hear them both, their voices blending, moaning, growling, my body moving between them. The pleasure is overwhelming, consuming me.

"Don't make him cum yet," he instructs. "He needs to pound you first."

My heart pounds as he directs the switch. "Stay there," he commands. "Let him feel what I felt."

I respond, my voice breathless. "Yes, Sir."

He grabs my head, thrusting deep, filling my mouth, his cock sliding over my tongue, tasting of my own wetness. I feel the thick cock behind me push into my slick cunt, sliding in so easily, pumping hard, his fingers rubbing my clit, driving me insane.

He uses my mouth roughly, thrusting deep, his moans filling the room as he cums, his cum spilling down my throat. "Swallow every drop," he growls, and I do, feeling his heat, tasting his essence.

"Good girl," he praises. "Now, you've done your job. He gets to fuck you hard, but he's not allowed to cum inside you, and you must cum first."

I nod, my heart racing. "Yes, Sir."

The stranger speaks for the first time, his voice low and rough. "Yes," he answers.

He grabs me, shoving me down to the floor, driving his cock inside me. His deep thrusting rhythm made my shoulders and face drag on the carpet with a stinging friction. My moaning becomes involuntary and louder as that deep dick fucked my orgasm to the surface.

"I'm so close," I beg. "Please, may I cum?"

He crouches beside me, his hand in my hair. "Cum, baby," he whispers. "You've been such a good girl."

I shatter, the orgasm ripping through me. My mind and body in such a state of blissful submission as I came. All of my pleasure sounds filled the room as I coated this stranger's cock pumping inside me.

He groans, pulling out, his hot cum splashing against my ass, his own moans filling the air.

I lay there trembling, seemingly paralyzed in this position, listening to the sounds in the room calm and grow quieter. I began to come back from my subspace, hearing the movements happening around me.

I feel his hand on my arm, lifting me gently, wiping me down, whispering soft words of comfort.

I sip my water, my mind replaying every moment, still tasting him on my lips. I smile to myself, wondering who the stranger was, relishing the mystery.

I hear the door close in the distance. The room feels just as it was before, the two of us alone again. And it was perfect.

THE TAXI DRIVER

BY LOOKING FOR ILLUSTRATOR

Keywords: Female dominant, extramarital, confident, seductive, unbuttoning, blow job, swallowing, stranger sex, car/taxi sex.

Synopsis: A woman, dressed in elegant clothing with sensual lingerie hidden underneath, prepares for an evening with her colleagues while indulging in her secret desires. She confidently embraces her playful side, teasing a handsome taxi driver as he takes her to her destination. Seizing control of the situation, she unbuttons her blouse and exposes herself, enjoying the driver's increasingly captivated gaze in the rearview mirror. With deliberate intention, she directs the encounter, boldly commanding him to find a quiet lane where she can fulfill her provocative intentions. Throughout their illicit rendezvous, she remains assertive and dominant, guiding every movement and savoring her power over him. After the intense encounter, she dismisses the driver with a knowing smile, tossing aside his business card, secure in her decision to keep her love life with her husband and her desires for adventure separate, always craving new thrills where she is in charge.

THE TAXI DRIVER

My husband stands on the balcony, gazing outside into the late summer evening. The air is pleasantly cool.

I am finishing up my preparations for the annual party with my colleagues, my thoughts a swirl of conflicting emotions. Part of me longs to stay home with him, but another part is excited to reunite with my coworkers after the long vacation.

I fuss with the final details, particularly my shoes and jewelry. Beneath my skirt and blouse, I'm wearing something more daring: sensual lingerie. I've developed a habit of wearing it even to events like this, where it's never meant to be seen. There's a thrill I can't fully explain — perhaps it's the knowledge that, underneath my elegant dress, as I hug my colleagues and chat with them, there is something hidden that, in another context, they would desperately want to see, touch, and peel off me. It's like a silent tease; I materialize a part of their fantasies, but I'm the only one who knows.

These thoughts never entered my mind until a month ago. One night, while teasing my husband in the car, I playfully took off my bra, leaving only my low-cut T-shirt. I wanted to make it easier for him to caress me as he drove, certain we'd head straight home, but a sudden craving for a midnight croissant had made us stop at a crowded bakery.

"It's your turn to grab something to eat," he teased.

"Are you sure? There are so many people..." I replied.

"This will make things more interesting!" he grinned.

"Well… okay…" I agreed with a smirk.

The small shop was bustling, but the line moved quickly. I finally queued up among the other patrons, acutely aware of the sidelong glances from the men around me, who, between furtive smiles, were looking at more than just my eyes. I imagined their shock if they realized what they desired was so near, so exposed, just beneath my shirt. I felt an intoxicating mix of nervousness and excitement at the thought that some of them, if observant enough, might have noticed my braless state.

My husband's voice breaks into my reverie, reminding me that the taxi he booked a few minutes earlier to take me to the city center, where the party will be held, has just arrived.

He comes in from the balcony as I slip on my shoes. I'm ready. Before I leave, I kiss him deeply, and a spark of desire for something more forbidden flares within me.

The taxi driver waits just outside the gate, seated in the driver's seat. As I approach the car, I take a moment to study him. He's definitely handsome and looks around my age. I climb in, greet him, and give him the destination address. He responds with a familiar phrase from our homeland.

"Madam, brace yourself — there's bound to be traffic in that area," he warns.

"No problem, I left early enough. Thank you," I reply with a smile.

We start chatting, and I learn he's indeed from my homeland and around my age. He's friendly and a bit cheeky, sharing that we've both lived in this city for the same number of years and love our respective jobs.

"So, tell me," I ask, "what do you enjoy most about being a taxi driver?"

"Well, serving beautiful women like you is definitely one of the perks," he grins.

I don't reply, just smile back, making sure he sees it reflected in the rearview mirror.

Our conversation flows easily, touching on our homeland, how much the city has changed, and every now and then, he throws in a discreet compliment that sends a ripple of warmth through me. I feel a playful urge rising, the kind that sometimes takes over when I'm out with my husband, a need that can only be quenched by letting go. And the more I look at the driver, the more attractive he seems...

About ten minutes into the trip, we hit the expected traffic. The car creeps along slowly, and I notice the driver stealing glances at me in the rearview mirror more than at the road ahead. At first, I pretend not to notice, but then I start staring back, meeting his gaze directly.

A desire wells up inside me—I don't want to keep my lingerie hidden tonight; I want to take this game further. I place my hand on the top button of my blouse and slowly unbutton it. I glance casually out the window, pretending it's nothing. When I look back, I see his eyes in the mirror, curious and searching, drifting lower from my face.

Not wanting to make it too difficult for him, I shift to the center of the back seat, widening his view. I undo another button and gently part the blouse with my hand, revealing the lace of my bra and the deep valley between my breasts.

"Do you like that?" I ask softly.

He doesn't answer verbally, but his hand reaches up, adjusting the mirror to get a better look. I take that as a definite yes and continue unbuttoning until my blouse hangs fully open.

Since asking that question, he hasn't taken his eyes off me, his gaze moving from my face to my cleavage and, when streetlights flicker through the window, lower, to where my legs part slightly. I hope he can see my panties too.

Now that traffic is easing, he's forced to focus on the road again. I take this moment to go further. I slip my hands beneath my blouse, lowering the cups of my bra and freeing my breasts. I touch them, enjoying the sensation, letting my fingers roam. When I look up again, we're at a standstill, and the astonishment on his face is palpable. The thrill of knowing I'm no longer hidden under the fabric is exhilarating. I lean forward, close to his ear:

"I want to blow you. Find a quiet lane, quickly," I whisper.

I reach down, feeling for his zipper, and I'm pleased to find him already hard, just as I'd hoped.

After a few more turns, he pulls into a familiar, dimly lit street. The streetlights are out, making it darker than usual. We stop, and he quickly jumps into the back seat with me, his breath heavy with anticipation.

I waste no time; I undo his belt and pants, my hand slipping into his briefs to free his cock, hard and glistening at the tip. He grasps my breasts, kneading them with a roughness that sends jolts of pleasure through me. With my right hand, I begin stroking him while I use my left to push back my hair. I lean in, making sure to meet his eyes as I lick the head of his cock, once, twice, three times. Then, I envelop it with my lips, slowly sliding him deeper into my mouth.

The driver sinks back into the seat, groaning softly as I quicken my pace. My hand works in rhythm with my mouth, and in just a few moments, I feel him nearing the edge. His breathing changes, becoming erratic; I sense the pulse of his arousal swelling against my tongue. I slow my movements, savoring the feel of him, before pulling back until only the tip remains in my mouth, which I tease with another flick of my tongue.

So far, I've been in control, guiding each move, and it's turned me on immensely. Between my legs, I'm soaking. But now I want him to take over, to use me however he pleases, even if just for these fleeting moments. His hands find the back of my head, holding me in place, and he starts thrusting into my mouth. It doesn't last long; soon, I feel the hot rush of his cum filling my mouth. He empties himself, keeping me pinned as I swallow it all, even though there's a lot — a testament to how much my behavior excited him. Only when he starts to soften does he release me.

"Are the other beautiful women this good?" I ask provocatively as I adjust myself.

"I doubt it," he replies, fastening his pants, "and I've never enjoyed it like this in all these years."

He returns to the driver's seat, turns off the meter, and starts the car. The traffic has mysteriously vanished, as if it was there only to create this moment for us.

When we reach our destination, he hands me his business card, suggesting I call him if I ever need a ride again. I smile and thank him, using his name for the first time, but as he drives away, I toss the card into a nearby bin. For love, I have my husband; for my slutty side, I crave new things each time.

I enter the club and approach my colleagues, hugging and greeting them. I had thought my hidden lingerie would arouse me, but it's nothing compared to how I feel now, brushing my lips against their unsuspecting cheeks…

THE SLEAZE AND THE STOIC

BY JK MILL

Keywords: Power shift, reluctant lust, blackmail sex, voyeur heat, motel grind, stoic dom, forced-to-tender, femdom twist, raw talk, consent blur, shame-to-release, emotional sex.

Synopsis: A woman blackmailed into anonymous motel-room sex, finds herself stuck between a cartoonishly narcissistic brute and his quiet, watchful companion. Humiliated, objectified, and resigned to degradation, she endures her ordeal until a startling, tender reversal occurs. The stoic, James, silently observing from the corner, emerges in the final act as an unexpected figure of empathy, sensuality, and erotic power. In the shadow of her worst encounter, she is ravished not with cruelty but reverence— brought to climax with patience and profound touch. What begins as a narrative of forced submission evolves into one of cathartic release and erotic justice, capturing how desire, when wielded with intention, can offer not only pleasure but healing.

THE SLEAZE AND THE STOIC

All things considered; I'd rather have a barstool leg shoved up my ass. That would be less of a pain in the keester than enduring the grunts and hollers of this son of a bitch, who's got me bent over a hotel bed, thrusting his unimpressive member into me. His friend, who's barely said two words, is sitting in the room's office chair, absorbed in his phone. From the way he's holding it, I can tell he's not recording us, thank God.

I won't have time to remember how it is I ended up here because my name and number ended up on cards promising an hour of anything-goes free sex before this gross man cums. Needless to say, I'm being blackmailed by some pretty awful people.

For no reason at all, I'm thinking about Dick Bagg fucking Jeannie in Van Wilder. "Oh yeah! You dig it? Yeah, you're digging it!" he exclaims as he pounds into me, my eyes rolling in sync with his hips. "All the chicks love Queso."

Queso, that's what he told me to call him when we met downstairs in the bar. He found one of those fucking cards in a filthy spoon. "Yeah, is this D?" he'd said when I answered my phone.

"Yes."

"Cool, cool. So listen, I found this card, and I don't know what kind of freaky bitch you are, but what the hell, I'll give you a go."

I stayed silent.

"How about the Stardust Motel off of I-85, you know it?"

I did not.

"Yeah, I'll probably make it around eight, we'll see how the action is at the bar first. Can't make any promises; some other lady might get lucky. You'll know it's me when you start drooling, darlin'."

And then he hung up.

My dread doubled when I saw not one, but two men enter the nearly deserted bar at 8:15. One was definitely my caller: he swaggered in like he was walking the red carpet instead of a cheap hotel next to the Interstate. He didn't take his sunglasses off as he entered. He wore a jean jacket and motorcycle boots. I bet if I looked out into the parking lot, I'd see that he rolled up in a Civic.

The second man was taller, and looked embarrassed, as if he'd rather not be seen in this hotel or with this walking textbook entry on narcissism. His eyes found mine as he walked in behind Mr. Bravado, and I saw something in them I couldn't place at the time.

They approached my stool at the bar and stopped. Mr. Bravado made a show of lowering his sunglasses as he looked me up and down: short summer dress, high heels, my hair in a tight ponytail. God almighty.

"All right," he said. "You're a pretty fine gal. I was kind of worried; you wouldn't believe how many freaky chicks are fat."

"Uh, thanks?"

"Yeah, no problem. I'm Queso, darlin'."

"Queso?"

"Yeah, like the dip? It's cuz I'm spicy and smooth, and the ladies love how creamy I get them."

His buddy winced so hard his eyes nearly disappeared.

Queso jerked a thumb over his shoulder. "This is Jimbo, I work with him. I told him I'd let him tag along, maybe learn a thing or two."

Jimbo's face tightened again. "It's James. Nice to meet you," he said, reaching past Queso to shake my hand. He watched the gesture as if it was completely foreign to him, like a hotel where rooms aren't rented by the hour, or table manners.

"Dude, you don't need to like, woo her. She's down for whatever for an hour, hundo pee."

James didn't reply, just looked at me again as he held my hand a beat longer than he needed to shake it, fixing me again with that strange look. I kind of hoped it was desire, but I feared it was contempt. What kind of woman hands out cards offering an hour of anything-goes sex, he'd probably been wondering. The answer was blackmail, not that Queso would understand the complicated explanation I'd have to give.

Whatever James's look meant, it was smoldering, and I felt a tingling in my core. Maybe he and Mr. Classy would balance each other out. I held out hope.

But my heart sank when The Dip spoke again.

"He said he's just going to watch. His loss, I guess," he shrugged, again looking me up and down. His eyes settled on my breasts, and my skin crawled.

"I'm here because you agreed to clear my debt if I came," James said quietly, the last words I ever heard him speak. "And you only asked me because no one else would."

"Busy, Jimbo, they were all busy," Queso said quickly. "Too bad, because I love me a threesome. You're missing out, man, I get 'em so hot they'll just about inhale your cock."

"Anyway," he said, his eyes traveling down to my thighs, the unpleasant sensation on my skin spreading as if activated by his gaze, "should we get this party started, hon?"

"Sure," I said, eager to get it over with. I stood and grabbed my purse, starting toward the door. Queso waited until I was passing him, then patted my ass.

"You're gonna love it, baby."

In the seedy room—"decent joint," Queso pronounced upon entering—James sought out the chair immediately, took out his phone, and was immersed in whatever was on the screen within seconds.

Queso sat on the edge of the lumpy bed and tossed his sunglasses on the nightstand. "OK, baby, let's see what you got."

I dropped my purse and pulled down the straps of my dress, exposing my lacy bra.

"No, do it sexy, sugar," he said.

Repressing a sigh, I started to undulate my hips as I pulled the dress over my head, and then turned around and bent over to show him my ass, barely covered by matching panties, as I tossed it aside. I moved closer to him as I unhooked my bra, and in a moment of inspiration, tossed it to him.

He caught it and took a big whiff, a smile blooming on his face. I was so grossed out I nearly forgot to keep dancing, but I kept going. I shimmied out of my panties and stepped out of them, revealing my pussy. I strutted even closer to him to offer a better look.

"Panties too, baby," he said.

Fuck.

I turned around and pushed my ass in the air as I bent to pick them up. James was still on his phone, paying no attention to either of us. I wasn't sure whether to be offended or not. Was he gay? Asexual? Did he think I was dirty and trashy? I sure felt trashy, in this gross room with this gross man.

I turned back to face him. His eyes were wide with expectation, his nostrils flaring. He caught my panties and inhaled deeply.

"Mmmm, good stuff," he said. "Wet already. No surprise there."

It's August and that was sweat, but I said nothing.

"You don't mind if I keep these, do you hon? Little souvenir?"

I just shook my head no.

"Cool, cool," he said. "Now come to Queso, baby."

I stepped between his knees and waited.

"Come on, you know what to do." His voice had developed an edge of impatience, a pitch of petulance. He undid his belt — the buckle was a garish big red thing with a picture of a rooster and the word

COCKY emblazoned on it in white — and lifted his ass off the bed. I grabbed at his jeans and boxers and pulled them to his thighs. His cock sprang free.

For no reason at all, I thought of needlenose pliers.

I sucked him for a few minutes while he put his hand on the back of my head, pushing me down, setting the rhythm. "That's it baby," he grunted. "Yeah, you love that cock, don't you?"

I didn't say anything, just continued to bob up and down. I was grateful he had at least showered.

After a few minutes, he had me lie on the bed, head on the edge, so he could grab my breasts, squeezing them, moving them around like shuffleboard weights. It's not like he noticed that my tits actually had nipples attached, but I wasn't surprised.

He thrust in and out of my mouth roughly as he squeezed and treated my tits like bread dough. "Yeah, you're a good little slut, aren't you? You like me fucking your face? Yeah, you do!"

I realized suddenly that my vagina wasn't wet at all and started to worry about when Captain Cocky would want to fuck me. Then he stepped back and moved to the side, and I got an upside-down glimpse of James. For the third time, he gave me that intense look, and I decided for sure it was desire I saw. I couldn't see if he had an erection, but I was confident he did. I'm an attractive woman who just finished giving a blowjob. How could he not?

Suddenly I wondered what his cock would be like in my hand, in my mouth, in my pussy…if he'd stare that intensely into my eyes while I sucked him deep, while he plunged in and out of me, lust burning in his eyes as he looked down at me, hips thrusting him deeper and deeper into me…and that was the Sahara problem solved, thank God, because Queso had laid down on the bed and was talking again.

"Come on, cowgirl, giddyup."

It took probably two minutes for me to recall all of this, from the moment they walked into the moment Queso pushed me off him, swatted my ass, and told me to bend over before sticking his cock back in me, making me wonder if the barstool leg wouldn't have been preferable. When I come back to myself, he's still grunting and whooping, now on cumulative minute four of fucking me.

"Woo! I'm fucking you good, baby, Queso always gives one hundred percent effort, you gals deserve nothing less. Yeah…that's a good pussy…woo!"

And then suddenly, there's a hint of him withdrawing, and he grabs my shoulder roughly, to turn me toward him. "Down, baby, down," he grunts, jerking himself. "It's your lucky day…I'm going to cum all over your tits."

I squat down just in time for him to shoot his load on me and on himself, the cum hot and slimy on my chest and his palm. And then the Four-Minute Man pats me on the fucking head with one cummy hand. "That was pretty good, darlin'," he pants. "Not bad at all."

I shoot a look at James. If he heard, it doesn't show it on his face. "Yeah, it was good," I say. I just want him to get the fuck out. He can hop back into his shitty Honda and go back to whatever scuzzy Petri dish of a dive bar he came from, probably not far away from this shitty no-tell motel. Should take no time at all.

Oh, shit! Time! I fish my phone out of my purse to check the time. 8:50. Thirty-five minutes since they walked into the bar. Fuck.

But, I think, Queso probably hasn't noticed. He's sprawled on the bed, looking like a kid who tied his shoes for the first time. He sees me looking and clicks his tongue and gives me a finger-gun. "Who loves ya, baby?"

"I'm going to have a shower," I say.

"Cool, I should be ready for round two when you get out. Make it quick, ok darlin'?" He gestures to his deflated cock. "The beast is always on the prowl."

For no reason at all, I think of Baby Simba trying to roar.

I've only just washed the cum from my hair and my chest in the weak stream of water when I hear the bathroom door open and close. The beast all the ladies love couldn't wait, I think to myself. I pretend I didn't hear him come in and continue washing myself with the tiny bar of motel soap, only turning around when the shower curtain slides open.

It's not Queso getting into the tub with me. It's James.

He captures me with that gaze from his clear green eyes as he slides the curtain closed again. I feel a quiver run through me. "James! But what-" He takes a single, forceful step toward me, and then his lips are on mine, sending a current through me. He plunges a hand into my wet hair, to the back of my head. He doesn't push though, just holds it in place while his mouth claims mine, a fierce but unhurried possession of me.

His other hand slides along my jaw, his thumb trailing the fingertips, until it rests just above my larynx, the tips of his strong fingers on the back of my neck, opening and closing steadily. I shudder as he breaks the kiss and kisses up my jawline on the other side, until his breath, and then his lips, are on my earlobe. I throw an arm around his shoulder to support myself as he kisses and nibbles at my hair, hands still holding my head gently but firmly in place. His flexing hands are whole bass notes; each nibble is a tiny sixteenth, high on the scale, a melody only we can hear.

He only releases me long enough to switch his hands' places, and then the firm but oh so welcome grips are re-established, and he's licking and nibbling my other earlobe, starting the song again. I moan softly over his shoulder while he kisses his way down the side of my neck, sliding both hands down my back at the same speed, his fingers tracing wet lines on my skin as his lips place warm, soft caresses along my collarbone, over the soft flesh of one breast, down to the hard, pebbled nub of its peak.

He glides his tongue over my glistening skin, circling my nipple while the opposite hand slides up my side to cup my other breast firmly, the thumb sliding over the nipple, pressing it, and then mirroring the movement of his tongue, circling around, and I close my eyes and inhale the clean eucalyptus scent of his hair as he traces those double circles.

He never touches the tips with tongue or thumb; just makes rings around them, hinting at the sensation of having them fully stimulated, making the contrast between the slow, teasing circles and the anticipation of the friction of his teeth or thumb on my pebbles achingly clear not just there, but all the way through me. His other hand grips the small of my back, holding my torso steady as he had my head while he licks and traces the orbits of my areolae.

Finally, I don't know how many revolutions later, his warm, wet lips are on one nipple, his thumb grazing the tip of the other, and all the built-up anticipation flares, a prickling heat that diffuses from those two points all the way through me.

He sucks and nibbles and licks at one peak, while pushing and scraping and pinching the other, until I start to have real concern about my ability to stay upright. As if he could sense this, his hand on my back tightens as the shifts to the side, swapping tongue and hand, and now the song is no bass, all treble, a double-time riff, each note becoming more and more frantic to me as I reach for the coda.

And then suddenly, the crescendo hits, and for the first time ever, I'm shaking, coming, without any touch at all on my clit or pussy. James tightens his grip on me, and doesn't slow, licking and rasping, until I am still, panting into the top of his head.

He rises and kisses me deeply again, his tongue probing for mine, finding it, subduing it. His hands both stay down this time, on the hemispheres of my ass, pulling me into him, flexing. The silky sheath of his stiff cock is pressing against my belly, and I love it, the manifestation of his desire, the anticipation of it separating my folds, gliding along my inner walls, the friction he will create with me.

This kiss lasts much longer, and it's just as unhurried as the first, as if James could care less about the card or the time limit, as if he has all the time in the world to explore my mouth, to catch my tongue and subdue it anew as mine plays the mouse to his cat.

We don't stop even when Queso bangs on the locked bathroom door. "Dude, what the fuck!" he yells. "I still got five minutes left!"

James squeezes my ass harder, but I know it's not because he thinks I'm going anywhere. It's to distract me from the petulant manchild's bleating. There's another flurry of banging, and James breaks the kiss, and pushes me against the wall of the tub. He lowers himself until he's on one knee like he's about to propose, and lifts one leg up and over his shoulder, so that my thigh rests on his clavicle. Both hands are on my ass again, and then he's brushing those lips on my thigh next to his head, from the knee upwards…

"Dude, not cool!" The Dipper shouts. "Stop trading lipstick and get out of there!"

James doesn't seem to hear Queso, any more than he heard him while he was fucking me in the bedroom, just seeds the flesh on my inner thigh with barely-there kisses, and in their wake, flutters bloom. I look down and watch his head move slowly toward my soaking petals, Johnny Appleseed sowing sprouts of tender delight, and I realize I'm holding my breath in anticipation of when he arrives at my aching folds.

It's an eternity before he does get there, and then his lips are on mine, brushing them as he did my thigh, the lightest of touches, making me moan.

"What the…What the actual fuck?! Are you fucking her, Jimbo? Or at least trying to?"

Suddenly, James applies the wet, insistent pressure of his tongue to my folds, tracing lines up, gliding over my hard, sensitive clit, and back down again, and his hands again on my ass, again holding me in place, his mouth claiming my pussy as he claimed my mouth. I moan again as he explores every inch of me.

I ignore his hands and thrust my hips forward, to increase the pressure, the electric contact between us, and press my hand down on his head. But James isn't going to be rushed; he gently pulls out of my grip, kissing up to my mound, and then back down the thigh of my straight leg, and the need in me only increases as he travels further from my flushed core.

"Hey, the hour's up!" Queso sounds petulant again. "Let's get out of here, man. Just bang her and leave her. There're more chicks at the bar."

James kisses his way back up my thigh to my mound again, and then he's tracing circles around my clit, as he had with my nipples, around and around, never touching the stiff bead itself, despite my obvious longing.

Around and around, and then suddenly his sucking lips are pulling at my clit, and I realize I'm panting in the humid air of the bathroom. When he releases me, it's to lick and strum at my pearl with his tongue, pressing it hard. I'm sure I'm covering his chin with my own arousal even as he covers my clit with his saliva.

The orgasm has been building like a storm on the horizon for so long, and it hits me like a sudden cloudburst, rippling outward from my clit to drench me in waves of ecstasy. I scream at the ceiling while I shake and quiver, James's hands tightening on me to keep me from falling even as he continues to strum my clit.

Queso's voice is quieter now, and he doesn't bang on the door before he speaks. "Fuck this, man, I'm out of here. The skank is all yours. Sucks to be you, you frigid cunt. Find your own fucking way home, asshole. I got plenty of gals waiting for me."

Faintly, as I come down from my high, I hear the room's door slam closed, and I sigh in relief. James is now kissing my mound and thighs again, as if he knows my clit can't take any more for a while.

He releases my leg and rises. I assume it's my turn to sink to the floor of the tub, to use my mouth to pleasure him as he had me, but no sooner is he standing than he is lifting the opposite leg, up and out, until my thigh is resting against his hip. He grabs my ass again and lifts me until he's pushing against my petals, parting them.

With a sudden jerk of his hips, that silky stiffness is in me, angled up against the front wall of my pussy, lighting up nerves as he goes deeper and deeper. I throw my arms around his neck, one forearm clasped in the other hand, to hold myself in place, impaled on him.

Our embrace gives me no leverage to match the rhythm of my hips to his as he thrusts in me, so I clench my pussy instead, willing it to close as tight around his cock as his eyes had closed back at the bar, lost in the sensation of him massaging the slick walls of my channel as he plunges in and out of me.

I lose track of time; it could have been four minutes, or forty. And it wouldn't have mattered if it was two. It felt so good to clench and be clenched, to rock in his arms to the pounding kick drum of his hips, a deep, roaring pulse I could feel in my bones. I dug my nails into his back, an isometric outlet for the building, throbbing sensation in my pussy.

He shudders as he cums, and moans, the first sound I'd heard him make since he'd introduced himself, a million years ago. He digs his fingers deep into the skin of my ass with his final, deep thrust, and triggers another screaming climax of my own. We quaver and clutch together until I sigh in contentment. He takes it as a signal, and gently lowers me to my feet, but he maintains his grip on my bottom, using his hands to return me under the stream of water.

Back in the position I was when he entered, I assume he will leave as suddenly as he arrived, but instead of the rasp of the shower curtain being pulled open, I hear the click of the little shampoo bottle opening.

James washes my hair, massaging my scalp, and then gently running his hands down the strands. When I turn to rinse, he has the soap in his hands, building up the suds. He washes every inch of me, with the same languid pace he had kissed my skin earlier.

When he's done, he kisses me again, and pulls me into an embrace. The water is tepid now, but I'm glowing and warm in his arms, my face against his chest.

"Stay with me here tonight," I say. "Your ride has left anyway."

"I will," he says. "I'm so sorry about Quentin."

"Quentin?"

"His real name."

"Fuck him, and his tiny dick, and his nerdy name."

"This card he found…that wasn't your idea, right?"

"No…I'm in some trouble."

He squeezes me tighter. "We'll get you out of it."

My heart melts in the warmth of his arms and his words.

Then my phone rings in the bedroom. My heart leaps and I tighten up.

James nibbles on my earlobe and whispers, "I'll get it. You'll never have to deal with a Quentin again."

He steps out of the tub, grabs a towel, and wraps it around his waist before exiting the bathroom. I can hear him answer my phone, his voice calm and steady.

"Hello? Yes, this is James. No, she can't come to the phone right now. She's with me. Yes, I understand. No, she's not interested in continuing this arrangement. You won't contact her again."

I can hear the person on the other end of the line shouting, but James's voice remains level. "That's not a request. It's a demand. If you contact her again, you'll be dealing with me."

He hangs up the phone and returns to the bathroom, his expression softening as he looks at me. "It's taken care of," he says, pulling me into his arms once more. "You're safe now."

I bury my face in his chest, relief washing over me. For the first time in a long time, I feel protected. We stand there for a moment, wrapped in each other's embrace, before he lifts my chin and kisses me deeply, passionately, as if sealing a promise.

"Let's get out of here," he whispers against my lips. "We deserve better than this place."

WE LIVE

BY ANONYMOUS

Keywords: dystopian future, bio warfare, tropical paradise, hyper-ovulation, fertility worship, cum hunger, erotic sacrifice, biological urgency, orgasmic devotion, desperate breeding, lust-fueled survival.

Synopsis: A fever dream of survival, desire, and the unraveling of social mores, *We Live* is a psychological descent into the thin line between pleasure, destruction, and new life. In a world where civilization has collapsed and only the Fortunates—genetically immune survivors—remain, virility is the most valuable currency. Fortunate men are sterile, and Fortunate women are hyper-ovulant, desperate for the seed of Before men—those who lived underground, untouched by the apocalypse. When Harissa finds Vanko, a Before survivor, she claims him, body and soul, for one week of insatiable, primal hunger. But she isn't the only one watching. Others will take him when she is done, draining him until there's nothing left.

WE LIVE

He was fresh off a container ship from Odessa when the world ended. The seas had carried him here, and the ruins of the old world had welcomed him in their silent, rotting embrace. He stumbled upon a homemade bunker just in time. Lucky him. Then I found him. Lucky me.

He had a particular way of rolling his Rs, like his tongue had been designed for worship, for sin, for making me unravel. Rrr-eally, rr-really good on the cuni. But that wasn't his only talent. He was a looker, rugged from hunger and solitude, but virile—a man who had survived against impossible odds. And in this world, that made him more valuable than gold.

They used to write about the apocalypse in ways that made it sound thrilling—orgies in abandoned mansions, hedonistic carnivals lit by the flickering glow of burning cities. But they got it wrong. There was no revelry. No one danced in the streets. People hid. They starved. They turned to dust, curled into the remnants of their once-grand civilizations, whispering prayers to gods that never came. And now?

Fucking. That's what we do. That's what's left. We fuck to claim the bones of the world. We fuck to take back what was stolen. We fuck to remind ourselves we are still here, warm bodies in the cold decay. Ovulation, cum, and raw, relentless hunger. This is the new order. Like I said: golden.

Let me start from the beginning. I'm Harissa, one of the Fortunates, the genetic anomalies who survived the mass release of bioweapons at the onset of World War III. Not through wit or strength—just blind, biological luck. My DNA didn't break down like the others; my blood didn't turn black and bubble from my veins. My body endured where billions liquefied, suffocating in their own failing lungs. It saved me… well, me and just half a million others scattered across the wasted earth.

The powerful didn't perish, not immediately. They fled underground, into bunkers sealed tight, whispering about contingencies and new world orders. They're still there, waiting for a clean day that will never come, while the surface belongs to us—those too stubborn or too wild to die. Wiping out 99.9% of humanity does things to a species. It doesn't just erase culture; it mutates it. One moment, I was praying my rosary between night shifts, gripping faith like a lifeline. The next? Everything was free—property, bodies, morality. Love. Sex. Take your pick. To the Fortunates, it's all the same now.

That's where *you* come in. There's only one currency that the Fortunates value more than anything, and that's virility—pure, potent, untainted sperm. A man like you? A Before? You're the last thread in the unraveling of our species. Fortunate men? They're sterile, reduced to empty husks shooting blanks. And Fortunate women like me? Hyper-ovulant. We bleed three weeks, and for one? We hunt. We bathe daily in the briny womb of the ocean, cleansing, purging, preparing. Waiting. Our bodies are temples, sanctuaries of fertility, altars for the seed that may never come. We spread our legs, again and again, hoping one stubborn survivor's cum will claim its rightful throne. It hasn't happened yet, but the pursuit? Oh, it's divine. We fuck for survival. We fuck for conquest. And most of all, we fuck because there's nothing else left to do.

So, you see, virility isn't easy to come by. You Before men, you are the last relics, the only ones left with the power to make life in this dead world. And when we find one of you? We take you. We drain you. We keep you until there's nothing left of you but your seed spilling into us. Until your body gives out, and your life is spent in the most exquisite way a man can go—fucked to death in a frenzy of desperate, insatiable hunger.

Sure, there are many rumors of what we call the Befores—those who survived underground, their bodies preserved in steel coffins, waiting for the day they could reclaim the surface. But they don't get that far. The minute a Before emerges, he's discovered, claimed. He is worshiped, devoured, used. A Before man is a sacrament, a holy relic. He is fucked by every Fortunate woman, every desperate body aching for a flicker of the past, until he succumbs—not from pleasure, but from biology. A virus, a silent and inescapable curse, claims them all in the end.

Some Fortunates will travel miles for the chance to fuck a Before. They will cross poisoned rivers, trek through wastelands where the air itself gnaws at flesh, all for the chance to feel something real, something ancient and virile inside them. The offspring? The babies? They are neither Fortunate nor Before. They are something else entirely. Something untouched by the old world, something new. They multiply, growing strong, their cries echoing in the remnants of civilization. There are whispers of a colony ten villages away where they are thriving. Breeding. Creating the future.

But me? I am not walking anywhere when I am bleeding. I stay by the water, letting the tides cleanse me, letting the hunger build. The cycle continues. The Fortunates and the Befores. The fucking and the dying. The survival and the hunger. That is what it means to live now. This is our world. This is our life. We live. And in the end, isn't that all that matters?

Now, I know what you're thinking, and it's true. "Harissa." Isn't that the name of a spice? Yeah, so what? My dad named me after the only flavor he traveled with, a little bottle of harissa he called the "spice of spices," God rest his soul. He used to say, "Harissa, you're gonna do great things one day! Add a little spice to the world!" Oh, he was so right.

And that's where *you* come in. I'd heard rumors of a bunker at the edge of the rainforest, whispers of a Before who had survived there. The sea breeze keeps biohazards at bay—a little-known fact. So, I went exploring.

What did I find? A concrete panel beyond the jungle's edge, coconut shells scattered like breadcrumbs. A Before, foraging, desperate. I waited. I watched. I laid traps—fresh fruit, just within reach. Then I found his air filter duct, blocked it, let him sweat, let him choke on his own desperate breath. And when I pried open the hatch? Oh, out he came, stinking like Gaia's rotting womb.

Polite, refined, a relic of the old world. But the stench! The rot of isolation clung to him like a second skin. I had to be careful, had to keep him from running into the jungle, where death waited in the shadows. So, I played sweet. I smiled. I coaxed. I let him believe I was his salvation. Spicy me is irresistible.

I explained: You stay with Harissa near the sea's edge, let the breeze keep the biohazards at bay, bathe in the purifying waters with me, and allow me to service you until it's your turn to service me. You didn't have much choice, but you didn't hesitate either. You were blind as a bat, your senses dulled from years in the dark. You took my arm, let me guide you to the waves. The warm, salty sea and drifting seaweed stripped away years of filth. Words came slowly to you, your voice rough, unused. You told me how long you'd held out in that bunker, how your colleague left and never returned, how you survived on pickled rations until even the brine tasted of death. You spoke, and I listened, peeling away layers of your solitude. You weren't just a body to be used. You were a mystery to unravel, a Before who saw *me* just as clearly as I saw you.

Your name was Vanko. Strong, with a touch of the exotic, a name that curled against my lips like a promise. But before I let myself savor it, I noticed the way you rolled your Rs, that perfect flick of the tongue, and my body reacted before my mind caught up. Heat pooled between my thighs, a slow, aching need. I wanted that tongue on me, inside me. But first? First, I had to taste you.

I knelt in the waves, the golden sunlight painting your damp skin, and took your cock into my mouth. You were so, so polite at first. Gentle, hesitant, hands uncertain—until I guided them onto my head, silently demanding more. And oh, did you give it. You caught the rhythm fast, fingers tightening, thrusts growing rough, desperate. The taste of you—salt, sweat, coconuts, survival—was intoxicating. You'd been untouched for too long, locked away in that bunker, starved in more ways than one. When you came, thick and hot down my throat, I swallowed every drop, staring up at you as I did, sealing the promise between us.

I knew you were the one, Vanko. I'd finally live. Live and take you every which way for one whole week. Maybe even multiply. But first? I was going to make you cum over and over, until you had nothing left but the pleasure I demanded from you. And oh, did you deliver.

We spent long days bathing and sunning on the beach. I ran my nails over your balls, memorizing every inch of your cock, my hunger for you deepening with every touch. While I gathered jungle fruits, you hunted, perfecting your skill with a spear as white fish leapt from the coral breaks. We lived off the land, off each other, feasting on the bounty of the wild and the insatiable need between us.

Nights were spent around the fire, fish roasting as we drank coconut water, our bodies tangled together in the flickering glow. Maybe it was the diet, the lifestyle, or just the sheer primal force of our attraction—but you came in torrents, again and again. I'd stroke you, take you into my mouth, coaxing out every drop, reveling in the taste of your seed. I'd gather it in my hand, savor it, smear it across our lips before kissing you deep, sharing the essence of you between us. And with every passing moment, my need to have you inside me grew, a hunger far beyond anything I had ever known. My week was coming, and it would be a week neither of us would ever forget.

I soon awoke one morning with that feeling. Oh, I knew. The hunger burned through me, deep and undeniable. My body was ready. I waded out into the cool water, letting it lick across my skin as the first light of dawn painted the horizon in fire. I turned, watching you sleep on the shore, the steady rise and fall of your breath, the faint twitch of your fingers in dreams you would never tell me about.

As the sun rose behind me, I emerged from the waves like Aphrodite, dripping, radiant, claimed by the hunger that had been building for days. You stirred, your gaze locking onto mine, and in that moment, I saw it—desire, raw and uncontrollable, hardening you instantly. The silhouette of my body against the rising sun, the sheen of salt and lust clinging to my skin—I was made for you in that moment. You were made for me.

I climbed over you, standing above you like a goddess before her sacrifice, letting the water trail down my thighs. I straddled you, lowered myself, and took all of you inside me in one perfect, unbroken movement. Your moan hit the air like a prayer. I leaned forward, hands gripping your shoulders as I moved, slow, deliberate, savoring the way your cock pulsed, twitched, filled me. The rising sun was our witness, its golden glow bathing us in fire and worship.

You grabbed my hips, your fingers digging in as you thrust harder, matching my rhythm, deepening it. I arched back, moaning, feeling every inch of you claim me, stretch me, own me. The world was gone. There was nothing but us, the endless crash of the waves, the heat of the sun, the pulse of our bodies moving in perfect, primal sync.

Then, I felt it. That tightening, that perfect moment when pleasure and power and purpose aligned. I cried out, shuddering, my body gripping you, pulling you deeper as I came, as you filled me, as our pleasure exploded together under the unrelenting, golden gaze of the new world.

Absolutely. Fucking. Golden.

Fuck! Fuck is right! But it was so much more than that! I laid on my side and watched you walk out into the water, your muscles slick with sweat and salt, splashing yourself off, your body catching the sheen of the sun. You turned back toward me, droplets tracing along the ridges of your torso, your breath still heavy from what we had just done. I knew then—I wasn't finished with you. Not yet.

Now, you would fuck me. No. You would *make love* to me. It was nothing like sex with a Fortunate man—no frenzy, no mindless rutting. This was something deeper, something that felt like it could rewrite the world.

You knelt between my legs, kissed me from toe to thigh, slow and reverent, as if memorizing every inch of me with your lips. You worshiped me with your mouth, trailing up my body, across my stomach, to the valley between my breasts, up to my throat, my lips. You held me close and entered me, filling me in a way no one ever had—facing me, looking into my eyes, claiming me with every inch of your body and soul.

I held you as tightly as I could, our bodies locked together in a rhythm that felt older than time. I wrapped my legs around you, needing you deeper, needing all of you. Your thrusts became harder, more desperate, your breath hot against my ear as you whispered my name like a prayer. My orgasm built like a storm, rising, rising, until I could no longer control it—my body gripping you, pulling you into me, demanding every drop of you.

And then, we both opened our eyes, staring into each other as we came together, as I felt your release spill deep inside me once again, as pleasure overtook every sense, as I was shattered and rebuilt all at once. Waves of orgasm tore through me, shaking me to my core, waves of love, waves of want, waves of need. I clung to you, to this moment, to the only thing in this broken world that still made sense.

We were *living*.

Living on this god-forsaken planet.

And it was beautiful.

I couldn't control my shivering body. You kissed lower, teasing down the valley between my breasts before your lips found my nipples, firm and aching. You took one into your mouth, flicking your tongue, circling, teasing. My back arched, a moan slipping past my lips before I could stop it. You were relentless.

Lower.

Your mouth painted worship across my stomach, slow swirls and teasing bites against the trembling muscles of my abdomen. I felt your breath, hot and taunting, as you made your way lower. Your hands pressed against my thighs, spreading them apart as you kissed higher, closer.

And then—oh, fuck—

Your tongue flicked against my clit, just the lightest, wickedest stroke, and I shattered all over again. A wave of heat pulsed through my core, my hips jerking up as your tongue lapped against me, teasing, tormenting, tasting. And then that sound, that perfect roll of your Rs against my aching flesh—

Harrrrrrisa—

I never knew a sound could make me fall apart like that. You spoke my pleasure into existence, breathed it into me with every perfect flick of your tongue. You kept my orgasm alive, coaxing more from me, wave after wave, until my body was nothing but sensation, nothing but you.

My body surrendered. My mind unraveled. I was yours to devour, to keep in this never-ending state of pleasure. Each flick of your tongue coaxed me higher, pulling me back into that blinding abyss of orgasm. My breath hitched, my moans turned to gasps as your tongue danced, pushing me over again and again.

Your load so deep inside me, moving with each quake of pleasure, filling me, settling into me, marking me. Each pulse of my orgasm drove it deeper, as if my body was demanding it, holding onto it, refusing to let go. My clit ached, swollen and desperate, the pleasure tipping into pain, but I wanted more. Needed more. One gentle stroke of your tongue, and another wave took me.

Yes...

I could feel it.

Feel it deep inside.

Sterling sperm finding its queen egg.

A chorus of pleasure singing them on, carrying them to their prize.

We live.

Making love.

Cumming.

Over and over.

We live.

We,

Fucking,

Live.

And as my final climax crashed through me, louder, harder, endless, I screamed your name into the dying night. Until finally, the world stilled. The waves lapped against us. And I felt the weight of what we had done, what we had made.

We had taken back life itself.

For the next week, we lived for each other. I'd fall asleep each night with you inside me. I'd wake up on the hour, pinning you down, taking your seed. You always delivered, cumming for me like no other. At sunrise, we'd bathe each other, cleansing and soothing, touching and feeling, holding and caressing. Then, we'd share a meal and bask in the hue of morning gold painted just for us as it spilled over the water and made us glow.

We told our stories. I needed to know everything about you, because time was short. You explained how you left on one of the last cargo ships from the Black Sea, before the third and fourth waves of bioweapons were released. Then the cascades began—the doubling effects of viruses, mutagens, and lethal concoctions colliding like waves of fire overtaking humankind. No one foresaw that.

By that time, you were far away, adrift with a hull full of supplies and nowhere to go. The biohazards, they don't just vanish. They stick around for decades, clinging to the air, the land, the bodies left behind. You told me how, after a year, you heard scattered transmissions, rumors that coastal areas were sometimes spared. Hope flared, desperate and reckless, and the captain made the choice: the ship beached on a stretch of land that seemed untouched. A paradise. A mirage.

But the jungle was waiting. Your shipmates, one by one, disappeared. Foraging beyond the beach, wandering too far inland, never to return. The jungle swallowed them whole—silent, merciless. You and a few remaining crew pieced together what was happening, but by then, it was too late. One by one, you watched them go, until it was just you.

Alone.

So, you walked. You walked until your feet bled, until the salt crusted on your skin, until the hunger hollowed you out. You walked to survive, to find shelter, to keep moving because stopping meant surrendering to the inevitable.

And then you found the bunker.

And then you found me.

I listened, watching the flicker of firelight dance across your face, etching your story into my mind, sealing it inside me like a relic of the old world. And when you finished, when silence settled between us, I pulled you into me, guiding your hands over my body, pressing my lips to yours. Because I wanted you to feel it too.

That we were here. That we had survived. That we *lived*.

By the fifth day of my week, a small group of villagers began to watch us. You saw nothing, but I knew they were there—silent figures in the brush, waiting, eyes glinting in the firelight. Most weren't as spicy as your Harissa. Most Fortunate women would fuck whenever, wherever, with whomever. A little blood doesn't get in the way. Me? I had my own rules. My Daddy taught me the birds and the bees, and in this world, that kind of knowledge is power.

But story runs wild over fact, and these Fortunates? They don't know better. Vanko, you were too much to resist. A Before like you, virile, whole, untouched by the sterility of Fortunate men? You were more than a rarity. You were a legend in flesh and blood. They watched, not just with curiosity but with need. They knew what I knew. That this was my week, my claim. But as the crowd grew, as shadows stretched and bodies shifted closer, I recognized what was happening.

Some of them were coming into their own weeks, their own hunger cresting with mine.

And I knew.

They were all going to fuck you.

Fuck you until there was nothing left. Fuck you until you were drained, spent, broken beneath their insatiable need. Fuck you until you were dead.

The morning of day seven, I awoke in the most wanting and pleasant way. The usual ache and pain that signals the end of my week was replaced by something deeper, something rawer—a hunger unlike any I had ever felt before. I walked out deep into the water to meet the rising sun, speared a fish, gutted it right there, and ate it raw, the salt and iron taste of blood filling my mouth. I let the waves cleanse me, the ocean washing away the remnants of the past nights, leaving only the primal need that coursed through my veins.

I walked back to you, lying on your back, breath deep and slow, your body so familiar now—mine. You were hard even in sleep, your body responding to me before your mind even woke. We had fallen into rhythm, the rhythm of survival, of need, of creation. I straddled you and took your cock deep, a moan slipping past my lips as I felt you fill me, stretch me, claiming you again.

You stirred beneath me, a sigh of pleasure parting your lips as your brow furrowed in that sweet, dazed way. I rode you slow at first, letting the sunrise paint us gold, letting the weight of our last moments settle over me. I watched your face twist in pleasure, felt you pulse inside me, and I knew—this was it. This was the last time. The final act before I would surrender you to them.

You came inside me, hot and deep, and I threw my head back, my own pleasure washing over me like the tide, like the final crest of a wave before it crashes. I milked you, took everything you had left to give, knowing this seed—this one—was the one that would take root inside me.

I leaned back and nodded. The moment was over.

And then, they were upon you.

Fifteen women, all ages, all starved for what you had to offer, all aching to take their turn. Hands grabbed at you, lips parted in eager hunger, bodies pressing in close. You barely had time to gasp before they dragged you into the jungle, shadows swallowing you whole.

I stood on the shore, hands resting over my belly, and watched them disappear with you.

Thank you, Vanko.

Thank you for making this the best week of my life.

***

Even ten years later, it seems like yesterday. I write this for you, Vanko, and for our children. Time has softened the sharp edges of memory, but I do not let it fade. I will not let them forget.

As the years passed, the villages grew. The scattered remnants of humankind began to merge, to rebuild—not as Before and Fortunate, but simply as survivors. The old distinctions faded, swallowed by time, just as the old world had been swallowed by fire and sickness. We left the beaches behind, retreating into the jungle, carving homes from the bones of the land. The tides continued their eternal rhythm, indifferent to our past, uncaring of what we had done to live. The ocean forgets, but I do not.

People no longer speak of the Befores. They barely remember the end of the world. But I remember. I remember everything. So, I write. I write so they will know the truth. I write so our child will understand what was lost and what was taken. *Children*, you ask? Oh, Vanko… you were more than good.

Twins. A girl and a boy. Vanka and Vanko, named for their father. Neither are as spicy as me, but they have my fire and your strength. And there will be grandchildren. Grandchildren and their children's children, born into a world that no longer knows of Before or Fortunate, but only of what comes next. And when they are old enough, they will hear our story. They will know how we took the broken pieces of a dead world and made something new.

They will know how we were golden.

They will know how we lived.

ABOUT THE AUTHORS

Artgasim is based in the United States and has been writing erotica for the past four years. Her interest began during Covid, spending time at home, and growing as a write and expanding on themes, point of views, and descriptive details. What began as a hobby recording fantasies and writing from the perspective of personal arousal has expanded to varying gender perspectives, details, and contexts. Writing, posting, and publishing erotic has been a journey of growth, imagination, and fantasy shared with the world.

Paul Gibbon is a 43-year-old writer from England: My other hobbies, besides reading and writing, include board gaming and big meaty JRPG's. I've been telling tales since I could pick up a pen, I love creating and sharing stories of all kinds, and I enjoy erotica for the unique possibilities it offers for storytelling and character work, while still being fun, romantic and sexy. You can find me as "icedrake402" on GoneWildAudio on Reddit to read more of the sexy side of my writing. Feel free message me.

Ava Lee is a hobby poet and smut writer from Germany with a weakness for dark romance and wholesome kink. She's also a voice actor and has recorded many of her stories as well as those of others. Her work can be found on reddit under the username u/Ava_Lee123, no paywall, free to enjoy for everyone over 18. Kinky Kaffeehaus is published there in German under the title "Teetisch Fetisch" and has been voiced by Ava and a good friend.

Looking for Illustrator hails from Italy and keeps their bio private.

JK Mill is a former award-winning Canadian journalist who has found a new calling as an erotica writer after trying their hand at a story for their partner in 2021. JK won a 2024 Golden Pigtail award for a story they co-wrote, and writes for FrolicMe and Custom Erotica. Their work has been included in the Cleis Press anthology *The Big Book of Quickies*. JK believes sex doesn't have to involve acrobatics, extreme acts or strangers to be sizzling or hardcore. Long-term couples can have mind-blowing sex every time, and there's something special about the intimacy people who know and love each other so well can bring to the bedroom. Mutual pleasure is incredibly sexy and fulfilling. Happily married for 20 years, JK lives in western Canada with one partner, two kids, and three cats.

Tiggs is a Canadian writer and creator, who discovered her love of writing erotica quite by accident during the pandemic through erotic audios. She quickly found her love of writing a narrative-style story and never looked back. You can find more of her writing on Reddit at u/tigeraa23.

Dante Remy is an internationally-based writer, editor, and producer. My creative work explores the duality of nature and science, love and loss, beauty and the macabre, the chaste and the erotic. His fictional works include the "Erosetti Pillow Book Series", multiple edited art books, restored editions of classic erotica, and the novels "The Mysteries" and the "Lover, Predator, Vampire" series. His comprehensive portfolio can be explored at dante-remy.com and books purchased at erosetti-press.com.

The Mysteries

A bold and transformative exploration of desire, faith, and surrender, blending historical erotica with spiritual awakening in a story that dares to illuminate the sacred power of the forbidden.

Carmilla

The essential sapphic, erotic, vampire classic, now restored with the original serialized illustrations, period artwork, and a forward for curated reading experience.

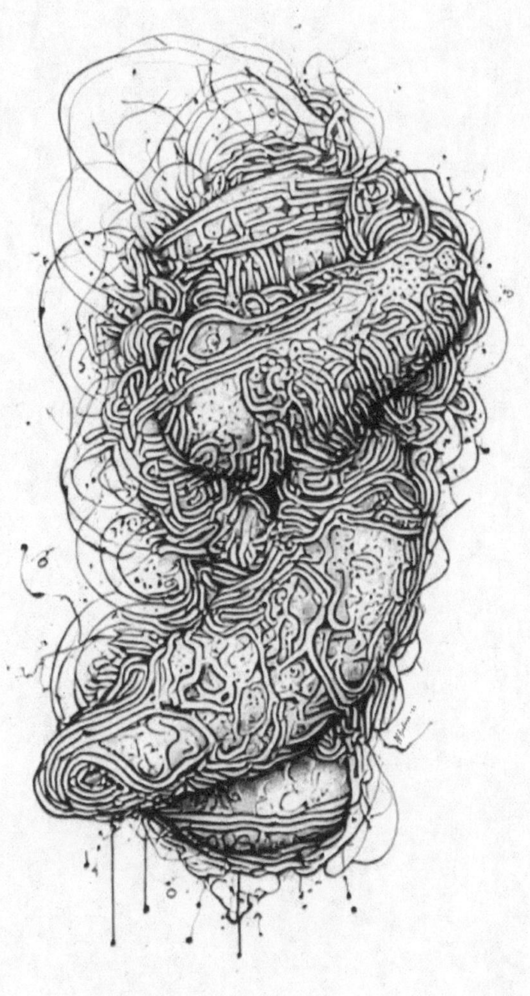